Penina's Letters

A Novel

Joe Linker

Penina's Letters is a work of fiction. Names, characters, places, or incidents are either the creation of the author's imagination or used in a fictitious manner, and any resemblance to actual persons, living or dead, businesses, locales, or events is coincidental.

Draft segments of Penina's Letters appeared in *The Boulevard* (Summer 2012), a publication of the Attic Institute of Arts and Letters. Parts of the "How to Surf" chapter appeared in different form on *Berfrois* on September 29, 2015.

Cover photo (1969), taken with an Exakta 500, is from the slide archive of Joe Linker.

~ Penina's Letters ~

Separation

On Television

Henry Killknot

Henry and The Punctuations

Holy Orders

On a Surfboard in Santa Monica Bay

How to Surf

Separation

"Bubo's problem no better?" Picul wanted to know.

"I don't know that Bubo has a problem. He just asked me to drop off this package."

"Don't jerk off with me, Persequi. I'm buried in paper, and I got Howler on my case, fit to be tied. Bubo got the clap, or what?"

"Love sick. He's been groaning in his sleep, something about a gal named Rhea."

"Ain't you a wise guy, Sally," Picul said, taking the bag I handed him and stashing it under his desk. "Tell Bubo to wrap his pipe in plumber's tape next time out."

"Bubo's sunk it in an ice pack for now. I think he's stripped the threads on the thing."

I walked back to the motor pool, where I found Bubo crying in the latrine. I sat down on a stool across from Bubo at the urinal and took out my notebook and pen.

When General Sherman suggested war is hell, he might have known what he was talking about. In hell, there are no indulgences. His march to the sea was not a surf trip, but hell is an idea too easy to explain and too simple an excuse. For the guys in Motor Pool Platoon, the war was purgatory, a fictitious place, where we washed and prayed, but where nobody got cleaned or saved. We waited strung out interludes between swells, indulging in packages from home or furloughs from the field spent in dives, and in smoke and drink, in liar's poker and in letters. All the fuss and hullabaloo, and a war just peters off. But none of that matters here. This isn't going to be about the war. I don't have any gory stories, nothing painting war as hell. Hell is an ocean with no waves. This is going to be about surfing and how I paddled out to live on the water after throwing Penina's letters off the end of the Refugio jetty.

"The pen is writing again," Bubo said. "The war is over, man. You can put the pen down."

"But I'm just getting loaded," I said.

"Haven't you already wrote Penina three letters today?"

"Your package has been delivered. Let's go to town."

"Ah, Jesus, I can't pee, Sal. Nothing's coming out. What did Picul say?"

"How long you been standing at that urinal?"

"I don't know. What time is it?"

"Freud might say you have a urinal fixation."

"This tail ain't no fragment of my imagination, Salty dog."

Beat Squad was part of the end surge ordering the last troops in from the field. My buddy Bubo Eyren and I lick-spittled through our last details, short-timers anxious to avoid pissing off Buck Sergeant Howler and Corporal Picul processing a backlog of discharge papers. But even the enterprise of retreat was given in military perspective the hurry up and wait treatment. We would go when we went. Meantime, the inescapable stream of rumors, details, and black market bartering – a full quart to clerk-typist Picul for the favor of cutting Bubo's orders showing he had passed the exit physical exam. Problems were sent to sick call, and names on sick parade were ineligible for discharge.

"I never saw a guy wrote as much as you, Salty."

"I've started a book. You're in it. You're going to be a famous character."

"I don't want to be famous. I just want to piss and go home."

Bubo stood at the clean white urinal, leaning forward, his sweaty head turned sideways with his cheek against the latrine wall.

"Please, dear, sweet Jesus, pray me an easy pee to piss from this pitiful penis."

"Picul said he was passing your papers up to Howler."

"Help me, Salty. God damn, help me. One pee, one clear piss is all I ask, and I swear I'll never peck this bad boy again."

"You feeling worse, Bubo?"

"My fuse is on fire, on fire! Sally, fire in the hole." Bubo's voice rose from a whisper to a yelp then waned with a moan.

"Hey, cool down, man. Let's go in to town, drink some beer. Drink enough beer, you'll be swimming in piss like it was the Missoula Floods."

"I'm dying, Sal. I'm dry as gunpowder packed in a paper hull."

"Let gravity work. The beer will be good for you. In vino veritas, in cervisia gravitas."

"Rotten hell."

"Come on. Let's go. The thing to do is keep moving. Don't go back to your bunk. You can't pee because you've got to prime the pump with beer."

Bubo backed away from the urinal, buttoning up his fatigue pants.

"My cock is a fried banana and my balls two dried figs, and all you can talk about is drinking beer."

In the end, the war wheezed and hissed, like foam from a frothy wave dissipating in mist up the beach. The rains had returned, falling mercifully onto the beach and into the tattered trees up from the water. Salvador Persequi and Beau Bob Eyren, buddies since Basic Combat Training, were now another couple of spent soldiers in a long line waiting to be sent home from a lost war. The squad slowed down, having not much to do but sit around and wait for processing. Bridge Platoon pulled maintenance on the pontoon bridge. Beat Squad was motor pool, mechanics, the compressor truck. Depot created jobs and details to keep us busy. We retubed split rim tires and hand packed grease into wheel bearings, painted the motor pool floor, policed cigarette butts and cleaned latrines, beachcombed for bloated bodies floated in with the tide.

The squad had moved from sleeping in the field, where the nights were cool and dark and open, to makeshift barracks for out-processing, where the nights were glaring and noisy and claustrophobic. But we kept getting passed by. In three weeks, no one had moved out. Rumor said we were not going anywhere soon because we were an engineer unit. We would be the last out, because of the bridge platoon.

An offshore lighthouse lamp flashed across the bridge and through the high windows of the barracks, thonging across the ceiling. Rest was offbeat. Come morning, we were tired. Evenings, we were free, and we usually walked to town to hang out and drink, but nights were full of sweats and dark swells, everybody waiting for something to break. Rumors crawled into bunks and kept guys awake scratching. The random, warm rain squalls did not bother me, and it felt good to be near the water again. We worked regular hours during the day, once all the equipment had been mothballed to the depot motor pool, but there was little work to keep us legitimately busy. Carpenter Squad built a coffin for Howler's dog, apparently the victim of an accidental overdose, a deaf Bully we called Underdog.

In town, we wandered from bar to bar and drank to excess, stumbling back after midnight, laughing or weeping, singing cadence in a parody of soldiering, dodging the MP's. Bubo started missing roll calls, but once our papers were processed, nobody would likely mess with us. We waited. The last few weeks had felt like a retreat from defeat, though no one said the words. Finally, we received our separation papers and discharge orders. Beat Squad agreed to hold together and wait for a commercial flight, but Bubo and I decided to ditch the squad and hop out. We spent one last night together drinking beer in town at the Orange Lizard Orchid Lounge. I saw Howler drinking with Picul and a couple of local girls. I nodded to Picul, who flipped me the bird, laughing in his beer, wiping the foam from his nose. I smiled and flashed Picul a waving peace sign. Howler was wearing pink and green cocktail umbrellas over his ears.

I climbed aboard a helicopter on Palm Sunday, the first of my improvised hops moving toward home, but it was too late for Bubo, who had turned himself in to the infirmary. He said he felt galvanized and had dreamt of taking a steel pipe cutter to himself. I flew a zigzag of military hops, crossing the ocean, finally landing in Fort Ord, where I hitched a ride into Salinas and up Highway 101 to San Jose and caught a commercial flight down to Los Angeles. I was still wearing the same grease stained, olive drab fatigue shirt and dungarees I had on when I said goodbye to Bubo six days ago and bugged out. It had taken me longer to hop back home than I expected. By the time I got to LA, I was dirty and unshaven and stiff from travelling cramped in payload and cargo bays. I had spent one peaceful night on the wood floor of an empty Quonset hut, my only light a slow motion moon through a few broken windows, and another night curled in the cab of a deuce and a half troop carrier, a family of feral cats having claimed the cargo bed. I had spent one sleepless night in a neon buzzing motel room and another in the hold of a humming prop cargo plane, the open ocean below.

But one thing I had learned in the Army was the useful skill of how to sleep. I had written Penina I could now sleep in private or in public, in a bed or on a floor, with blankets, in a bag, fully dressed including boots or naked, amid noise or in silence, in the dark or under a light, stomach full or hungry, head to toe or hanging upside-down from a chandelier. I could sleep under water if ordered to. But what I wanted now was to curl to sleep with

Penina. I didn't know I'd soon be sleeping with Penina head to toe.

I waited until I got close and called Penina from up north, rather than keep her on tenterhooks, and there she was, waiting for me at the gate in Los Angeles. Her bougainvillea red lips said, "Hi, Salty," and the soldier in me thought he might faint. I dropped my bag and hugged and kissed and smelled the pure and sweet Penina Seablouse. I held her face in my hands and rubbed her tears with my thumbs across her freckled cheeks. The phenomena of going to war and winning or losing a war seemed more uncertain than ever, and we had no audience. And it does not matter which war I had just returned from. It could have been any of them, including the next one. We waltzed across the terminal unnoticed, uncelebrated, and unphotographed. The only fanfare was the sound of cars that blasted us as we exited the terminal. Outside, the Santa Ana winds whisked up the awful Los Angeles exhaust. I tasted the heated air, a mixture of gas and asphalt and sea salt, and I told Penina I liked the taste, and I loved the smell.

The airport was jamming, very jazzy, cars cutting into the inside lanes, cars triple parked at the curb, traffic cops waving and whistling cars away that were not immediately loading or unloading passengers, a looping loudspeaker voice calling out the cadence. Tall bus shuttles from the local hotels jockeyed for position with honking yellow taxicabs hoping for a long drive up into the hills. Skycaps opened and closed doors, moving bags to and from stuffed car trunks and shaky-wheeled carts, and pocketed tips with a proud, expectant nod with no note of surreptitiousness.

If anyone took notice of us, we got no comments or looks, nary a glance, all about their own business. I pulled Penina close for another long hug, still no cameras shuttering, as if there had never been a war. We were a common couple. I had survived a war, and Penina had survived waiting. Whatever wounds she had yet to show me, her hair still smelled like baseball card bubblegum. I smelled of wheel oil, track grease, and sweat, my worn fatigues tainted from motor pool prattle, but Penina pressed her face against my chest, and I felt her take a deep breath. She rattled my dog tags playfully, and we fell in with a group of civilians waiting at a light and crossed the street. Penina pretended to help me walk through the parking lot, my arm around her shoulder. I stowed my duffle bag in the bed of the truck, and Penina drove us out of the airport, through the long tunnel under the runway, out Imperial, and down to Vista del Mar and the Pacific Ocean.

"The plane flew over the water and the beach coming in," I yelled, but the pickup truck was not a deuce and a half.

"We turned on the Santa Ana winds for your homecoming," Penina shouted back. "The planes are turned around, but why are we yelling?"

"I saw where the Airport Authority bulldozed my Dad's place. Looks like they've wiped out the neighborhood."

"I wrote you they moved the house, relocated a lot of them. But for sure we can't park out on the street and smooch there anymore, unless we want the Airport Authority peeping in on us." Penina fluffed her hair over her shoulder, laughed, and reached over and grabbed and squeezed my thigh.

"Those empty lots surrounded by chain link fence, be a good spot to set up a beach anti-assault force."

"It's okay, soldier. You can relax now," Penina said. "You're home. And you can stop talking so loud. I'm right here. You sure look like you just came from a war, by the way, and you smell something extra oil fishy salty."

"Yeah, two years of war and six days on the road, you know. So where is everyone? Why only you to meet me at the airport? Wanted me all to yourself?"

Penina ran her hand through her hair and said, "Only me? That doesn't make me feel very special."

"So there's the peace sign," I said, running my fingers across a decal on the back window. "But you didn't mention this one. Puck's Surfboards," I said, reading backwards.

The green, 1949 Ford pickup truck Penina was driving

belonged to me. She had pasted a little blue and white peace-symbol decal to the rear window, and she called the Ford the Peace Truck. She had written me a letter describing the decal. She had given the truck a name and asked if I was offended, worried I might not appreciate the peace symbol, but I had assured her I had no problem with peace signs.

After the tunnel, Penina turned west onto Imperial, and we felt the Santa Ana wind gust up and shake the truck. I planned to rebuild the engine and keep the truck in good running condition. My discharge pay would last some time if I could live with Penina, and I planned to shape boards at Puck Malone's surfboard shop, and Henry Killknot had solicited me to attach to his local National Guard unit as a special correspondent, and though it was a freelance idea, I hoped I might continue to land some articles. And I had the money my folks left me, though my father had sagely set up the trust like an IV with a slow drip. My father, who had survived two wars to become a successful architect and property developer, had never given me much advice, but he once said that desire is not synonymous with valor. He thought the heated mind malleable, and that strength comes from keeping one's cool. But I had seen frozen minds snap under the squeezing pressure of the cold.

"Will there be a soldier's home parade?" I asked.

Penina said something I did not catch.

"What?"

I had mentioned in a few letters to Penina what I called my sound effects, but it would probably take time for her to adjust to this eerie peculiarity. It wasn't just that I had lost some hearing, but I had noise in my head, whistles and dull echoes. Sometimes my head felt like a canyon, sometimes it seemed like a transistor radio, or I heard the sound of a guitar amplifier plugged into my ears, humming, and a screech of feedback leaving me momentarily stunned. I had talked to a medic who gave him me a field hearing test. The medic said it sounded to him like I had asymmetrical, fluctuating hearing. "Wear your ear plugs," he said. I decided to let the matter drop.

"I don't want to see any of the guys just yet," Penina repeated.

"That's good," I said, "that's cool," shrugging. "The sooner I get down to the water the better. I don't need to see anyone."

"Oh, don't start pouting, seasoned soldier," Penina laughed, reaching over and punching my arm. "Puck and Henry have planned a surprise for you up at Puck's surfboard shop. Try and act surprised."

"I am surprised. I'm surprised to even just be here. And

you are my surprise," I said, and Penina combed a hand through her hair, glancing in the rear view mirror.

"I need to shave and get cleaned up. I don't want to show up looking like a barbarian."

"I'm sure you were a perfect gentleman through most of the war."

"It's because I decided to hop out rather than wait for the commercial flights to arrive. There was going to be a lottery to see which platoons boarded early and got out first. A few guys, in no hurry to get home, or no home to get to, were already speculating how much they might make scalping their seats. The camp was chaos. There was a small window to hop out."

"Could anyone hop out?"

"If you knew an effective clerk-typist, one of the most powerful positions in the army."

"What happened to Bubo?"

"I left him in the infirmary, in bad shape. Maybe they requested a medevac. They stripped off Bubo's uniform and strapped him to a stretcher. I took one last look and saw some ancient nun trying to insert a catheter."

"Poor Bubo."

"Cruel war. You could get opiates on the black market cheaper than penicillin."

"The guys want to see you in your uniform. I thought you'd be wearing your dress uniform when you landed."

"I gave my stuff away, dress uniform, insignia, medals, to some local girl hanging around the bars. I think she was on her way to a masquerade ball."

"That sounds like an interesting story."

The light at Center Street turned yellow and Penina downshifted the three-speed on the column and braked the truck to a stop.

"I wanted to travel home light, because of all the hopping. I thought I explained that in a letter."

"No."

"The mail wasn't reliable toward the end. Hey, hang a left, go down Center, and we'll drive through El Segundo."

"We've got to get to the party," Penina said, and when the light changed, she continued down Imperial toward the ocean.

"Or Main Street. Let's drive down Main Street, past Library Park."

"You know we'll see someone, and you'll want to stop and say hi, which is fine, but they're expecting us at Puck's place. Besides, you stink like a red tide."

"I love the smell of the red tide."

"Why don't you tell me all about the girl and your

uniform?"

"Leah was her name, and she was giving my uniform to Bubo. He had misplaced his."

"Maybe I don't want to hear the story of the girl and your uniform."

"I'll tell you all about it later. I'm excited to be nearing the water. I can smell the ocean. I'm in love, Penina."

"You always were lovey-dovey romantic, Salty."

"You saved my life, Penina."

"Don't say that."

"Why not? You kept me sane."

"But you said you're not the same guy, so whose life did I save?"

"How about you? You the same girl?"

"You left a girl on the beach two years ago, Salvador, to fend for herself. And I didn't have a buddy like Bubo on hand to watch out for me."

At the end of Imperial, Penina turned the truck south onto Vista del Mar for the drive along the beach to Refugio. To the west, flattened by the winds, hunkered an ebbing Santa Monica Bay. Two red and black oil freighters were anchored off shore, one deep in the water, the other high, and three blue and white yachts appeared to be scurrying back to Marina del Rey. Above the horizon, the setting sun spread orange spears through the tar slick winds, and the smeared sky above with the windswept water below looked like an oil painting by Rothko. The Santa Ana winds had been blowing for a couple of days, and all the silt from the basin bowl had blown out over the water. It was Holy Saturday, and I thought I picked out the moon waning pale, high up, out over the water, but the Santa Ana winds were blowing, and I might have been seeing things. Close in, the beaches were buffed clean and empty, the waves flat, and no surfers were out in the water. The wind was now to port, blowing tumbleweeds across Vista del Mar, and Penina gripped the steering wheel with both hands.

"The truck's handling fine," I said. "Thanks for driving."

"Welcome home, Salty," Penina said. She was crying. She looked back at the road, and we drove on and up into Refugio.

Refugio was an unincorporated enclave of improvised alleys packed with dilapidated beach pads, situated between Vista del Mar and the ocean, a downhill triangle bordered by an El Porto base south at 45th Street and running northwest to a point near the jetty at the end of Grand Avenue, a distance of about one mile. At the point, near where the boardwalk ended at the jetty, filled with sand and ice plant, leaning away from the prevailing onshore winds, sat the wreck of the Refugio, at One North 52nd Street. We drove past the wreck, continued up Vista del Mar, turned right onto Refugio Road, and drove down the hill to Penina's place.

Penina lived in a single room, with her cat, Castus, above a garage in an alley. Refugio was dense with such non-compliant with codes living spaces. The garage was attached to a weatherworn beach house that belonged to Puck Malone. Puck was a capable surfer, a waterman, and an entrepreneur. He had opened a surfboard shop in Refugio, and his boards were popular. The shop was housed in another battered beach house, a gathering place for locals and surfers on surf trips looking for a crash pad. Penina squeezed into her parking space, too small for the truck. I got my bag out of the bed, and Penina pointed to a two-story apartment across the alley and said, "That's Henry's place." We climbed the outside stairs up to a small deck off Penina's door.

"You have a razor I can use? I don't have one." Castus, Penina's red-orange tabby, rubbed up against my leg, her back arched, and sniffed around my bag.

"There's stuff in the bathroom, in the medicine cabinet. Use whatever you need. I'm going to give Castus a treat."

"You know, you could jump in the shower with me."

"I don't want to get my hair wet."

"You'll look just fine in a shower cap."

"I'll wait out on the deck."

I shaved using cream and a double edge of Penina's,

showered, and put on a clean pair of dungarees and a flowered shirt I had traded with a helicopter pilot for a field jacket on a short hop in the islands. Penina had gone back out onto the deck. I stowed my stuff in a corner of the room and went out onto the deck to join her.

The warm wind was blowing down the streets of Refugio and out over the beach, but the deck faced west and was somewhat protected. There was a table and a couple of beach chairs out on the deck. Against the wall was a pummeled, three-cushion couch, its arms worn and soiled, tearing at the ends of the rests and cushions. A tangled, beachcomber shell-and-driftwood mobile rattled against the railing. In one corner of the deck spilled a pile of empty beer bottles held back by a couple of giant candles burned halfway down. On the wall next to the door hung a tool with a rusted, pointed steel end with a swivel flange fastened to a long and thick, weathered wood handle.

"What in the world is that?" I asked.

"That's my harpoon," Penina said.

"Thinking of going whaling?"

"Not in the water."

"You find this on the beach?"

"Storm surf washed it in."

"It's a log roller." I rubbed my hand across the smooth

21

wood of the handle. "It must have drifted down all the way from up north."

A surfboard was strapped to the deck rail.

"Whose board?"

"Puck's," Penina said, glancing about the deck, as if looking for something.

We had no time to waste before we were supposed to walk up to Puck Malone's surf shop for my surprise soldier's home reception.

"Whose idea was it to have this reception at Malone's so soon after you picked me up at the airport?"

"Everyone wants to see you," Penina said. "Puck and Henry were going to come to the airport, but I said I would meet you alone, and we'd come right up, and I promised them you'd still be wearing your dress uniform. Where did you get that crazy shirt?"

"I'm going to tie my last uniform in rocks and give it a sea burial. But how about another kiss first?"

"Can't that wait until later? Though you are looking sort of handsome again."

"I've been storing up a bundle of letters for this day, waiting for you."

"I know, I know. You made love to me in your letters.

22

You were as big and hard as a quivering kazoo."

"A kazoo? Did I say that? I must have been kidding. A kazoo is actually a comparatively small instrument."

"Your balls trembled like twin hummingbirds."

"You remember that?"

"It doesn't make any sense."

We kissed again, but Penina put her hands against my chest and pushed and pulled and wrestled away.

"Listen," Penina said. "I met you at the airport alone for a reason. I wanted to tell you something before you saw anyone else."

"What?"

"I'm sorry, Sal, but I did not wait."

Penina tried to grab a letter away from Puck Malone, but he was in a bully mood, and her protests fed his appetite for a tease. She looked around as if to go after another letter, but the letters quickly spread around. It would be hopeless and humiliating to scamper around trying to scoop them all back up. Penina retreated to my side, and we sat quietly and listened to the letters I had written to Penina while away in the war being read aloud at the reception.

"Penina, I love you," Malone sang out to an encouraging

23

cheer.

"I want to go surfing with you and get married," Malone continued. I glanced at Penina. She had her head down, combing her hands through her hair.

"I want to lick the salt off your cheeks when you come out of the waves," Malone read, but as he continued, the playful but sardonic tone went out of his voice. I recognized the letter as one of the first I had sent Penina after I had left for the Army. Malone's false tone mellowed as he struggled to maintain a sarcastic voice while simultaneously discovering what the letter was saying.

"I want to lick between your toes," Malone read, pausing as he scanned what was coming next, "and lick the soft part of the arches of your feet and around your ankles and lick up your calves and tickle your thighs and trace your triangle and stick my tongue in your belly button and tickle until you giggle, 'stop, stop, stop,' wiggling to get away but wanting more."

Malone paused to gulp and swallow a swig of his beer.

"This is some salty dog stuff, Sally," Malone bellowed.

"Were there no hurry, I would marvel," Malone continued reading, "as the poet Andrew Marvell said three hundred years ago, two hundred years at each breast, or until the oceans again cover the earth, but here comes the drill sergeant with his whistle

24

blowing his two minute warning so I'm on to your neck and brush your lips and lick the salt from your cheeks and close your blue eyes with my mouth and bury my face in your sun bleached hair. Got to go now. Love, Sal."

"What god-awful mush," Malone guffawed, to cheerful chortles, and he balled the paper up and tossed it over to Penina. She looked up and saw the ball of paper flying across the room and flinched as it hit her in the head and bounced to the floor.

The audience clapped and sent up a cheer after each letter, but applauding for the reader, the writer, Penina, the end of the war, one another, or the Easter Bunny, I wasn't sure. The reception had turned into a party. Probably the cheer was for the eclectic, free and easy present. Albums of blues and jazz spun through the evening. We drank from coffee cups and tumblers filled from a large keg of beer in the kitchen. When someone went out or came in through the front door, or the revelry paused as an album was changed, the Santa Ana winds offered a reminder, blowing over and down off the dunes and through the Refugio streets and alleys down to the beach and out over the ocean, that responsibilities floated in the offing. But not to worry, it was a party, and on it turned, into the night.

"Should we be reading these private letters aloud?" Henry Killknot addressed the audience in general.

"Oh, I think they're dear," Peggy Ann said.

"What was that one about a drill sergeant?" John Humulus asked.

"Never you mind," Mary Humulus said.

"Who's Andrew Marvel?" Lucas Crux asked Penina.

"I'm marveling at these war letters, Salty dog," Puck Malone said.

"It's Sally's feting," Henry Killknot said in a loud, commanding voice, standing to address the general assembly, waving his arms about the room. "We are deep into a mythical festal surf feast for the soldier home, a postwar party game, Salvador's resurrection from the war. Another letter," Killknot called out. "Who will read the next letter? I will!"

It's duck soup to suggest there were but two kinds of men in my generation, those who went to war and those who stayed home. The crucial question is what a man is to be, not what he has been, and how he experiences what he is, which is to say, the stories he tells about his life, if he tells anything. Most men are at least somewhat surprised when seize the day targets them with an "I want you." No matter how much he may have been expecting it, some part of him is caught off guard. I was not impressed with argument, whether a guy went or stayed, wanted to go but could not, did go but did not want to go, went gut full of gung ho or hog-tied squealing. Of interest now was what happens if and when he went but returned, and that answer had to be unfolded. It did not surprise or matter much to me that Penina, as she said, had not waited. Waited for what? I could see a scalpel cutting across my skin, just below my navel, but I felt anesthetized. I could not feel the knife. I tried to reach for it, but my arms were tied down. I must have passed out.

Puck Malone was a surfer who stole waves, who took off in front of other surfers and cut them off. He had all the trappings of the local surfer hero, and the young kids apparently looked up to him, but he had no respect for what I foolishly described as the secret heart of waves. I thought that while Puck enjoyed surfing, the surf did not bring Puck joy. So I was not thunderstruck to learn that while I was away at war Puck had paddled about on top of Penina. The blast of the letters I had written to Penina being read aloud at the party may have taken me off guard, but only in that I was concerned for Penina's feelings, and I had not expected to come home to find Penina's emotions in such disarray.

I had been an indefatigable letter writer in fatigues, and there were plenty of letters to go around at the party. But how did Penina's letters get to the reception? Was it a spontaneous, misbegotten idea, or someone's calculated prank? I did not think Puck had seen any of the letters prior to the party, but Puck

27

Malone was a trickster. The letters appeared out of nowhere and got passed around and read aloud, the music twirling within while the Santa Ana winds moaned down the alley outside. Penina looked beat. Someone put Miles Davis's "Kind of Blue" on the stereo and set the turntable to repeat, and I kept hearing the "So What" cut over and over again.

Puck and Henry seemed intent on lampooning Penina's letters. But Peggy Ann, one of Penina's friends, said, with apparently no irony intended, that Penina should publish the letters. One of the letters sparked an applied ethics argument, something about the value of the war and what would become of all the refugees, which almost ended in a fist fight. Puck wandered off, now bored. But letters kept popping up, the reading of the letters continuing sporadically, providing nourishment to the party. The letters gave the party a focus, created community, fostered purpose. Someone read a letter, a conversation ensued, the commotion died back down, and another reader was up, usually spurred on by Henry Killknot. The reading of the letters became a kind of party game, never mind the invasion to my and Penina's privacy.

Puck came back into the room, handed me another beer, his eyes red and dilated, and slapped me on the shoulder. "Good to have you back, Salty. See you and Penina together again, at last.

28

It's been hell not having you around to pester me into the water. We got to talk shop, though, got all kinds of orders for boards waiting, but there's time. I want you to take your time, get acclimated and all."

Puck turned his attention to Penina. "How you doing, Penina?" he said, grabbing her leg above the knee and tickling.

"Don't touch me," Penina hissed, pushing his hand away, and Puck jumped up laughing, kicking his legs out in a clumsy dance.

Henry Killknot pushed after Malone. They were arguing about opportunities to make money from veteran housing loan repossessions.

Small waves of partiers washed up, jostling in and jiving out. I leaned over and asked Penina, "Who are all these people?"

In the army, one got used to everyone looking pretty much the same. Uniform. One was one of many ones. Here, at the party, people appeared dressed somewhat uniformly but as if in costume. There were surfers in blue jeans and white tee shirts with girls in tight pedal pushers or bright paisley bell bottoms, hodads and bikers laden with boots and belts and chains, embroidered vests and leather jackets, jocks in shorts and polished tennis shoes and long haired stoners in huarache sandals. It might have been a Halloween costume party. Most of these trick or treat carousers did not stay long. They seemed to be looking for something they did not find. A few other veterans showed up, but they did not seem to have much to say to one another or to me. I did not seem to have much to say to anyone except Penina.

A police car stopped outside, blocking the alley, its red lights flashing. Puck and Henry went out to talk to the cops. After a few minutes the red lights went off and the car pulled away.

My coming home was an excuse for Puck to throw a party, not that he or anyone needed an excuse. After all, the war had indeed finally come to an end. I was tired. I might have passed out again, or simply dozed off for a spell. I was thinking about guard duty. Someone was asking me to read one of Penina's letters. Puck refilled my beer cup and handed me a letter. I stood unsteadily, hand clapping lightly smacking my ears. I looked at the letter. I could not decipher the words. A horizontal nonsense doodle decorated the page. It might have been a drawing of an M1 rifle. An f faced an l. The f looked like a soldier wearing a steel pot poking out of a foxhole. An h from the cavalry could not get by a line of x's and y's fixed to the page like hedgehogs in a field. "Who wrote this?" I asked. I dropped the paper to the floor, took a sip of beer, and improvised a letter, speaking directly to Penina.

"Dear Penina," I said, and paused. The room was quiet. Even the wind outside seemed to have died down for the moment.

"Your star sapphire blue eyes are about to squelch. Here is an extemporaneous, ignoramus, ignoble, silly prose poem of some sort. Oxymoron, that, like police action. No, wait, that's not oxymoronic. That's a you piss on their ism. But speaking of pissing on them, I'm thinking I'll piss on these letters. I'm standing tipsy at my soldier's home party at Puck's place, out of uniform, out of place, out of sorts, out of it, far out, right on, left faced, flooded with your letters, wading in letters written home, swimming in letters of incomprehensible doodles, listening to letter bombs fizzle, drunk on the potent purple ink of love letters. But how did all these letters get here, and with whom will you sleep tonight, my dear Penina? Love, your serviceman, Salty."

I turned from Penina to face the party and took a bow amid cheers and confetti falling from the ceiling. Then someone yelled Penina should read a letter, but we had not noticed she had suddenly slipped away.

The party crested and broke and people tootled off. A last letter was read by a blushing, hush-voiced hipster. I did not recognize the letter as anything I had ever written. Someone had finally let Miles finish his set. The candles and incense sticks were burnt down to their nubs. But Puck and Henry caught yet another wind, and at Henry's coaxing, a few bitter end partiers, led by Malone, Henry, and Peggy, walked in a mock solemn procession out of the surf shop.

Henry Killknot had collected the letters up and put them back in Penina's box, and I was carrying them down to the Refugio jetty. I had announced my intent to toss the letters into the ocean. Everyone thought this was a splendid idea, a morning Easter parade down to the beach. Penina may have been aware of the small procession walking from Malone's shop down to the Strand and down to the jetty, but she did not join the parade. Malone had brought along an ornamental tiki torch that he could not keep lit in the wind. It was about a mile from Malone's shop on 47th Street down to the Strand and north to the jetty, and by the time we got there, a fog-like sobriety had fallen over the group.

I walked out onto the jetty alone, the Santa Ana wind blowing at my back. I climbed down to a rock near the water, and one by one I threw Penina's letters off the end of the jetty. The papers fluttered about noisily in the wind and like afflicted birds fell into the waves.

It was past midnight when I got back to Penina's room. She let me in, but we had to sleep head to toe, an awkward arrangement of hers she had early introduced to me as punishment for causing hurt feelings. But it was just this kind of characteristic in Penina that I found endearing and one of the reasons I loved her. I might have suggested a foot rub to try to sweeten her mood, but the skin behind my ears that first night back was as dry as the brushed beach beneath the Santa Ana winds. I fell asleep thinking about waiting, waiting for the war to end, waiting for Bubo to pee, waiting for hops home, waiting in the water for waves, the wind blowing me out to sea.

By morning the winds had died and the water was glassy and there was a small swell, and even though I had been awake late, I awoke early and grabbed Malone's board from Penina's railing and walked down to the beach and paddled out. I thought of walking down to 42nd Street, but knew it would be too crowded. I could see a few guys catching wave shoulders rolling off the Refugio jetty. I paddled out at 47th where I had a wide section all to myself. I paddled out past the break, turned, and sat on Puck's board, looking back at Refugio and around at the Bay. I paddled back in and caught a few small, inside waves. I did not stay out long. I was sitting on Puck's board on the beach above the water line watching the water when Penina came walking toward me south from the jetty.

"How was going back into the water for the first time?" Penina said.

She sat down next to me on the surfboard in the sand.

"You missed it. I was born again. Of course, I had to baptize myself."

"Serves you right. Look, I found one of the letters washed up," and she held out a ball of wet pulp wrapped in seaweed string.

"They were gifts to me, every letter, and every one full of grace that I was saving for your return," Penina said.

"They were party favors last night."

"So what," Penina said. "What do you care what Puck Malone thinks? I hate him."

"I care what you think, and I care about what you've been through. I was caught off guard. I was surprised. I got a little emotional, not to mention not a little drunk. And you do not hate Puck Malone."

"I'm sorry, Sal. I was going to tell you. I wanted to tell you. But I didn't want to be one of those girls who writes a Dear John letter. And you told me not to. Remember?"

"Yes, I do remember saying no Dear John letters. And we decided not to get married. That was the deal."

"But it was a one time thing," Penina said. "A mistake."

"Why was it a mistake?"

"I wanted to talk about it before I slept with you again, so there would be no misunderstanding. And that letter you made up last night. That disgusting poem, or whatever you call it. Do you even remember what you said? In front of everyone. Then you go and do this," she said, holding up the fragment of the wet letter.

"What was the poem about?"

When Penina was upset, she shook her head and ran a hand through her hair. Then she was like a seal going under, and you never knew where she would surface next. She shook her head now, dropped the letter and ball of seaweed, and ran both hands through her hair.

"It was no fun being alone and feeling alone and feeling afraid of feeling alone and getting pestered and bothered everywhere I went, a special target, you know, the girl waiting for her soldier. Someone told me some asshole said, 'Penina always did have a cute face.'" Penina's voice rose and fell in small swells. She was near tears again, or had she already been crying this morning?

"It wasn't much fun being a soldier, either."

"I was like a trophy," Penina said.

"A solid gold weekend."

"A girl gets tempted, and, yes, seduced, and sometimes she succumbs. And once she falls, there's a brawl and a free for all."

"What do you say to we just turn the page on all that, and I'll write you some new letters?"

"Life is not a book, Sal. In a book you can throw my letters away and write new ones, but not in real life. You could have stopped them last night. Malone was being a jerk, but he respects you. Why didn't you do something? Why did you get up to read? Why make up that ridiculous letter poem to me? It was a mockery, what's the word, a parody of the real letters, making a joke of your love letters, letters to me, my letters, private letters, full of personal stuff. Why did you let it go on?"

"You can do things in a book you can't do in real life. Last night was like something in a book, a bad book at that."

"I felt so alone last night. Sitting next to you just made it worse. Who does that?" she said, kicking at the wet pulp of letter on the sand. "Who invests so much writing love letters to his girl and when he gets home throws them away into the ocean?"

"Some character in a love story."

"I loved your letters. I looked forward to them. I worried when a day went by and the mailbox was empty. I saved them in a special box. I wanted to read them all with you when you came home. It's something I thought you would like. I always thought we'd go down to the beach when you got home and sit on the sand watching the sunset and you would read your letters to me. I wanted to hear your voice close to me."

"Sounds lovely. How do you think your letter box got to the party?"

"I know you just got back from the war, and I'm worried

36

about you. And some of your letters hinted at something being wrong. Your ears, I know, something about your hearing, but that doesn't explain last night's behavior. Why didn't you do something? Why didn't you stop Puck and Henry last night? And why did you get up and help them make a fool of me? You could have stopped them. You could have said no. Some soldier you turned out to be."

Penina was not yelling. Her voice was soft. We were not fighting. We were both disappointed, in one another, and in ourselves, and in our friends.

"How has our sweet sorrow turned so sour so suddenly?" I said.

"Were you embarrassed? Is that it?" Penina said. "A guy survives a war but gets embarrassed when a bunch of drunk friends joke around with his love letters?"

"No, I was not embarrassed. Surprised. Interested in reactions."

"I used to sleep with them."

"So I heard. Like Trina with her gold coins. Weird."

"What?"

"Never mind."

We watched a line of seven brown pelicans gliding in single file over a swell.

"I used to sleep with your letters, fall asleep, and wake up with the pages falling from my hands. Sometimes, in the middle of the night, I would get up and listen to the surf out the open window, knowing that you were awake and working on the other side of the ocean, and I ached to have you there with me, but I'd think, he's writing, he's busy right now writing a letter to me, and thinking of you writing made me smile and gave me comfort and I'd get back into bed able to sleep. That's the grace I'm talking about, the grace of sleep, and of waking up in the morning rested and with something to look forward to."

"Yes, but I'm home now. Why do you still need the letters?"

"They made me cry but also laugh and filled me with hope and made me feel good about myself." She was shaking her head and running her hands through her hair. She looked trapped. Penina was a tough young woman but not unhappy and almost never cried. Salty comes back, and she mewls and pules. We were sitting on the surfboard, watching the waves, and she turned away. Was she crying again?

"They were just letters, paper, a soldier afraid in the dark whistling to himself. You can't make love to words. And here I am."

"Is that all you care about? Your tossing the letters off the

38

jetty told me you were so disappointed in me that you don't respect me anymore. And that insulting poem you made up told me that you don't really care about me. I'm just some fantasy to you."

"That's not why I threw the letters away."

"Then why did you throw my letters away?"

"I don't know. Why didn't you come down and stop me?"

"Wouldn't that have made a lovely scene."

"I didn't just dump them into the water. I sailed them off the end of jetty, into the wind, one by one. I should have put them into chronological order first."

"And now you're just like all the rest of them. If you still loved me, you wouldn't still want me."

"What? Have you come deranged too? Non compos mentis."

"What am I to you now, now that you know your pen pal's pen sprung a leak? Look at me. Why are you laughing? And now you are laughing at me?"

"Let's go up. I'm hungry for some hash and eggs."

If the image of pages of my letters falling from Penina's bed as she drifted to sleep warmed my soldier weary soul, there was no getting the letters back. I had written to her every chance I got. Writing the letters had been a lifebuoy. Penina was my diary, my journal. She was a book of psalms, songs of celebration, the creation of a first person plural, a we, yet there was nothing so mysterious or unusual in her being my reader, my constant companion, my pen pal, as she said. Even the roughest of hardboiled soldiers moves away disappointed from a silent mail call, yet I had not saved a single one of Penina's letters to me.

I had listened with a curious, detached interest to the letters read at the party. But I felt sleepy and after a few quick beers felt submerged. Someone had said something was nonsense, and I think I nodded in agreement. Someone had asked me what something meant, and I said I was not sure. They offered their own interpretations. I had nothing to add or subtract. In many of the letters I simply talked to Penina. I wrote as if I were reading a story to her. I drew pictures for her, sent her doodles, crazy drawings. I told her stories about the war, described the setting, the locals. I told her about my buddies, where they came from, what they each seemed up against. I told her nearly everything there was to know about Bubo. But these were not the letters that much interested anyone at the party. Henry Killknot rummaged through the box for something more.

I heard my voice complaining about the food, the details, the kitchen police duty, and the nightlong perimeter patrols. I was telling Penina about an overnight pass, a night out on the town. But this was not the letter the partiers wanted to hear, either. I was for a time in my letters to Penina a technical writer, describing the equipment, the land, and the work. But after several months of these letters I did not dwell on military maneuvers anymore. I did not want to relive the day in writing that I had to go back out and encounter again the next day. I had grown bored of writing the standard G.I. bill of fare, and I discovered and started to concentrate on the love letters, inventive and reflective love letters. And those were the prizes in the party game. Henry Killknot had Penina's box of letters on the floor between his legs, and when he found a good one, he let out a shout and picked someone to read it aloud.

The letters recalled me to the place and time of the writing, and Penina to the place and time of the reading. The letters were not so much about the war as about what it felt like to be away from home and at war, about missing and waiting, about fear and desire, need and want, risk and prize, crisscrossing back and forth the boundaries of hope and fantasy and despair and reality. The letters were also about what it might feel like to be home waiting. Penina understood that, but comprehension is a tricky trade. I looked at Penina. Why had the obvious purple patches of my war pen ink stung her skin like rubbing alcohol

41

when those letters were read aloud? I had not realized how serious the letters had become to her. I had been unaware of the consequences of my writing them. Had I written them for her, or for myself? Had I thrown them away because they were mine, not hers, and they now served no useful purpose? My letters had put Penina on the proverbial pedestal, and for her, they put me on a pedestal, too. I wrote the letters to Penina, but I also wrote them for myself. Penina's letters were momentary escapes from the war zone. They only made sense to me in the act of writing them. Of course I did not keep copies. I had not read and reread them as Penina had. I had not collected and collated them, adding newspaper clippings and photographs of the war to the collection. Often, mornings, I was away, Penina walked down to the beach, one of my letters in her pocket. She collected sand dollars, sea urchin shells, tiny fragments of smooth driftwood, and pretty agates. Then she sat alone on the beach and read and reread the letter. The letters I had written and the letters Penina read may not have been the same letters. What is written is often not what is read.

My letters to Penina contained ambiguously erotic language framed by funny anecdotes. Many contained private jokes between Penina and me, with words full of personal connotations. Maybe I had used Penina, and was glad to have an excuse to toss the letters once my need for them was over. I had told her repeatedly how much I missed her and loved her and wanted her, how I fell asleep thinking about her. But all the guys said these things in their letters home, or something like them, and it wasn't enough simply to make these statements. The clear statement seemed a kind of façade. What was behind the statement? I needed to find a way to express my thoughts and feelings using language that suggested, evoked, aroused and seduced, tickled and caused pain while allowing for hope. And these were the love letters Penina wanted and the love letters they wanted to hear at the party. Someone must have planned the reading of the letters at the party, and it was a smash hit. But love is different for the soldier away at war, alone in a sleeping bag under a shelter-half, than the lover back home, in a bed made whole with another. Away, out of earshot, a soldier's words might be aimed at targets both real and imaginary, while for the sendee, the letters fill a void the soldier, once home, cannot satisfy. The void fills with a sudden apparition, and the letters become a source of embarrassment, regret. They may contain vestiges of one's fear or cowardice. There were many passages I might want to redact. I might as well destroy them all.

In the weeks and days before I had left for the Army, Penina and I had spent every day and evening at the beach. The

43

acoustic surf, the hum of the water, concealed the sounds of the city behind us, and the sun disappeared without our noticing. We came out of the water like sea lions and rolled in the sand, bumping heads, necking and kissing as the tides rose hissing in the warm evenings and the cool nights, and in the morning I would get up early and surf while Penina slept. We did not talk about the war or about my having to leave soon, but as we got closer and closer to my induction date, something in me changed. I was sick with dread. I did not want to go. But my not wanting to go may not have had much to do with Penina. I was simply afraid. She sensed that fear, and my fear made her afraid. We began to worry.

"Greeting," the order from the draft board said, reclaiming grace like a landlord with an eviction notice, recovering his private beach. My pending induction forced a bittersweet fear to our time together, and I tried to recapture that bitter sweetness in my letters to Penina. Once into training and suddenly the noise and smoke and sweat and darkness of the war, I canoodled my fear. Each letter to Penina was my last letter. I saw guys vomit into their steal pots before going into the field, but they got the job done once the mission was underway. Penina was my steal pot. Call that fearful feeling butterflies, like a baseball player gets waiting on deck for his turn to bat, but in war they are more like birds tearing into the bowels. There is nothing worse than waiting for certain things while being torn apart by raptors of worry. This is how men are hollowed out. The hollow man does not worry, but neither does he love.

But paradise too is a compound where life in time grows monotonous, and after awhile, even the love letters trying to recall our bittersweet, last hours on the beach became monotonous, while the war was uprooting my senses, and I wanted to show how my mind was being ripped from its childhood sea. The war was a riptide pulling me away from Penina. My desire for her grew the further she receded, the further I drifted into the war zone. The uprooting of the senses, the tension of love growing in reverse proportion to its object receding, written in a context of risk and danger – this was the kind of thing Penina was thirsty for, and those were the letters they most wanted to hear at the party at Malone's, the same letters I happily and foolishly tossed from the jetty.

Penina did not think she could forgive me for the loss of her letters, but what made making up even harder for her was my lack of remorse. I did not seem to care about the letters, other than being interested in the scene of their being read in public. My throwing the letters into the water off the jetty was proof that I had used her. Somehow, Penina had interpreted my tossing her letters into the ocean as throwing her away.

But something more than the drowned letters doused our homecoming dreams. An emotion neither of us recognized rose like the onset of a strange illness, and we were not sure where exactly we hurt. There was the issue of Puck Malone, and of the suggestion that Malone had not been the only free and easy surfer to paddle into the surf on Penina's bed. At the party a few of the drunken locals had to be shushed when they started punning on Penina's peace truck. But they were surfers who did not actually surf much but talked as if they were big wave riders. Malone had followers who drafted in the wake of his popularity and success. I had been Malone's best friend, and that was their ticket to the homecoming party. They were Puck's surfer groupies. He tolerated them for the sake of his business interests. But even Puck probably had his limits, and he would not have countenanced another surfer cutting in on his wave. In the end, he would have protected Penina from others but also from himself. I knew that Puck had never been in love, and I knew that he did not love Penina. I concluded my mistake was my misjudging the importance of the letters to Penina. She had taken the letters seriously. They gave her a sense of pride, but she did not need to share them with anyone, and having them read in public confused her pride with shame. She lived alone, and she worried. She waited tables and tended bar for stoned surfers and drunk refinery workers. She was lonely. She yielded to their coarseness, a hardness she enjoyed. The refinery workers reminded her of her father. They smelled like her father. He had abandoned her, but she still loved him, or wanted to love him. The letters made her righteous, mended her heart and filled her with love. It is possible she would have been content were I to stay away permanently, like some troubadour poet, as long as the letters kept coming. My coming home put an end to our romance nurtured of longing and fear and worry and desire and valor.

"I feel like you threw me off the jetty last night," Penina said. "So what now?" she asked. We were standing on the Strand, up from the beach, looking back at the surf.

"Henry said last night he got permission for me to ride with his Guard unit on their next weekend drill."

"Why do you want to do that? Aren't you finished with the Army?"

"It's a chance to continue some purposeful writing," I said. "That writing I gave that reporter, Kidman, the guy that joined my squad for a month, loaded down with cameras, that writing got some attention."

"But they were his articles, not yours. And now you're talking about a weekend campout getting drunk with Henry

Killknot's National Guard unit? You call that war correspondence, wasting time with a bunch of weekend warriors?"

"It's an opening, that's all. A cross is a cross is a cross is a cross."

"You should have saved my letters if you wanted some war correspondence."

"That's not the same thing."

"You should sing your own songs."

"What does that mean?"

"Puck said you guys are planning a surf trip," Penina said.

"We might go up north, north of Santa Barbara, camp on the beach. You want to come? Or maybe we'll go down to Mexico."

"Who else is going?"

"I don't know, Humulus, probably, if Mary will let him go, and Lucas, and Henry."

"And Peggy and I along to cook and clean up," Penina said with a grimace. "I was hoping some things might change when you got back. Then what? What are you going to do with your war experience? What are you going to do with your life?"

"I don't know. Maybe I'll paddle out and live on the ocean, if I can't live with you."

"Why don't you seem very upset with me?" Penina said.

"You're a beautiful young woman, alone, no family. There's no disgrace, no shame. But you seem uncertain, and I'm not sure that's only because of the letters. It will take time to adjust to my being back, for both of us."

"I don't know what I want," Penina said. "I'm not the girl of your letters, though maybe I wish I was, or could be. She's too perfect."

"Are you serious about Malone?"

"What do you mean?"

"You slept with him more than once. He didn't park his board on your deck for a one night stand."

"Don't say that. I just need more time. Suddenly, here you are, an apparition. I can't make love to a ghost."

"Did you think I was not coming back?"

"One week's dead. And another week's dead. And another. And a day with no letter, and another day and still no letter. Then a letter would come, but after reading it, I'd think, maybe this is the last one, his last letter. Every letter sounded like it might be your last one."

"You thought I was not coming back," I said.

"I think maybe we should take some time to get to know each other for who we are now."

I was between thinking the whole affair of the letters, my writing them and tossing them and Penina's reaction to her love's letters lost, was tender and honest and a valuable illustration of longing and love, and thinking it was mawkish and sentimental and mulching in mush. There had been plenty in the letters to laugh at and to lampoon and ridicule, and it is natural and to be expected that a sarcastic set led by someone like Henry Killknot or Puck Malone will twist upper lips into grotesque sneers and mock holding hands and romance and tender but sentimental values, as the severe critic despises the improbabilities of purple prose, as the militant atheist scorns religion for giving people false hope, as the Christian rushes to clothe the exposed pagan baby, because so much of life is filled with false notions of love that disperse when tear gassed with experience. Purple prose is a façade. Behind the prose structure stretches a flat plateau peppered with tumbleweeds. Prose should work like a surfboard. But my experience of soldiering had taught me something of love as patience and forgiveness. I was weary of strategy and aggression, of sleeping with a loaded weapon by my side. I longed now for peace, peace and silence, and I knew peace was a virtue born of love, and I knew I could drown the sounds in my head, echoes from the war zone, in the ocean surf. Whatever else it is, love is not a façade.

I needed a place to sleep, and I wanted to sleep with

Penina, for when I was away from her, I missed her and wanted her, and I thought this feeling of missing and wanting, of longing, was what we call love, and so I thought I still loved her, so I wrote her a new letter, my first attempt to replace the ones I had thrown off the jetty. Here is that first letter:

Dear Penina,

I'm sitting complacently on your Santa Ana wind storm-strewn deck, and you're in the shell of your room, still sulking. Perhaps a letter will cheer you up, though you've said the ones I threw back to the ocean can't be replaced.

The first letter I wrote to you from the Army would have said something about how I was sorry I hadn't written yet, but they didn't give us a break the first three days, and at the end of the third day they suddenly sat us down and forced us to write a letter home, so the folks would know we hadn't been killed yet, I guess. They wanted to avoid moms writing to their senators. So they gave us pen and paper, one each. On my left was a kid out of Odessa who said he did not know how to write, so he dictated a few thoughts to me, and I wrote his letter for him. We addressed it to his mother. The guy on my other side was from somewhere in Arkansas, and he could read and write a little, but he could barely spell his name, so I helped him with his spelling. By the time I finally got around to writing something to you, Drill Sergeant Haett yelled out a two-minute warning. And that's how my first letter to you came to be written so short and sweet. You remember that first letter I sent you after leaving for the Army? Coincidentally, or maybe not, I think it was the first letter Malone read aloud at the party last night.

I don't want to think about the war, and I don't want to hear anything more about the letters. I just want peace and quiet. You asked me what I want to do with my life. I want to surf in the morning, work hard through the afternoon, write in the evening, and be with you at night. I don't want to sleep with letters. I want to sleep with you. I'm not looking for perfection, and when we fall, we should help one another.

Toward the end of the war we were rushing to get some refugees to a safe place. This was about three months ago. We were loading refugees into the back of a troop carrier, mostly women and children and old folks. The refugees were trying to decide which of them would board first, be the first into the first truck. There were only three trucks, and obviously not enough space for everyone. We were yelling at the parents and they were yelling at one another and the children were all crying. Time was running out. We had to get them into the trucks. We had to evacuate the area. But things were not moving. We had to take charge, and we started throwing the refugees into the truck, inadvertently separating families. The yelling grew to screams of confusion and fear and mistrust. The first truck pulled slowly away, and the next truck started to roll, both trucks packed, and out of the back of both trucks, arms and hands gestured helplessly, waving. You haven't heard screaming unless you have held a toddler whose mother is moving away in a troop carrier holding her arms out reaching for her child while others are holding her to keep her from jumping out. Packing the third truck was the worst. It was now inescapably clear not everyone would be rescued. Finally, the third truck was packed and started to pull away. There was a young woman hanging over the back rail, holding a child in one arm, her other arm waving down to someone stumbling behind. She seemed to be both waving goodbye and waving to come on, jump, climb in with us. The trucks were moving away. The refugees left behind stood in the wake of the trucks, watching. A man fell. Or maybe he simply dropped. I tried to help him up, but he didn't want to get up. He was groaning into the ground. I watched the woman in the truck with the child bring her hand to her face. And she reached out again, and she brought her hand to her head and pulled her hair, and on her face was a look of fear and panic, a look of sickness, of anguish. She kept covering and uncovering her eyes with her hand, biting her bottom lip, covering and uncovering her eyes, looking but not wanting to see. I jogged closely behind the truck for a little way, thinking she might jump out. The trucks picked up speed, shifted out of low, and I stopped running, and I watched the trucks turn on to the main road, and I could hear myself breathing and felt my heartbeat pounding in my ears.

While my squad was loading the trucks with the refugees, the bridge platoon was pulling up their pontoon bridge, and we now went to help them. This all took place in the morning and into the afternoon, packing the refugees off and the hard physical work on the bridge. By evening I was back in my compressor truck with my buddy Bubo and we fell into convoy with the bridge platoon. We drove through the night, stopping only once, to refuel. Our mission to rescue the refugees occurred over a three-day period, and I was not able to write you a letter. I did not even think of you much during those three days. I slept only a few hours in three days and three nights. I was losing my senses. I could still see, but the war had become a silent film. Perhaps it was then you were tempted and fell to the mercies of Malone, after successive days of reaching into an empty mailbox. I see you under Malone, reading one of my letters, not enjoying that much his lust for business, and I see that woman's face in the troop carrier, but she's no longer reaching out, and she's not watching me.

An ocean separates us still. I used to think of swimming away from the war, of carving a surfboard from a cedar tree and paddling across the ocean to you. It seems I'm still paddling, an oceanic Pony Express surfer carrying your letters to you.

I did not know the woman in the truck, but I cannot forget her. I slip back into that scene so easily, and I'm not here, not with you. I'm back with her, with the woman in the truck, jogging behind the truck as it pulls away, thinking she might jump. And it seems I don't know you, not the you of now. I have this memory of you, of our beach and ocean. I don't know what to do with that memory. And I don't know what to do with that memory of the woman pulling away in the truck.

I once asked Malone how long he thought he could tread water. "Three days," he said, joking, but I believed him. I don't envy Malone that he doesn't need a reason to do anything other than for fun or money, and while he could tread water for three days, he never would, for it wouldn't be any fun, and there would be no money in it. How long do you want me to tread water for you? I'll tread water for you until I drown. I'm out here treading water now.

Love, Sal

~ ~ ~

55

On Television

The water at El Porto those spring mornings I first got home looked like lead ladled from a plumber's melting pot, blue and grey and silver, a thick jellied glass. The air was soft and spongy, and cloud ear fungus floated quietly overhead like light sculpture. Close in, the swells rose and peaked and broke into soup rising like steam and soared up the beach in airy pillows. The sound of the surf filled my ears, drowning the dull drone in my head. It was very peaceful on the beach, near the water and the surf.

One morning, I was walking along the Strand, and I watched a few surfers down on the beach waxing their boards. One of them was Lucas Crux, another South Bay local and a friend who had been in the war. He had broken both his heels hopping out of a helicopter in the dark. At Malone's party, I had noticed a sober Lucas listening carefully to the letters, but he did not read one. Lucas had been back about six months now and was still walking, because of the bad heels, as if he could not decide which foot to favor. I watched from the Strand as Lucas's group paddled out into the surf. Soon they were out past the break and turning to get into position, taking off and dropping into the beach break waves quickly on their short boards. The trio of surfers worked the waves, the water full of flush, hissing horns. In lulls, they sat on their boards or paddled about a bit, watching for swells. One of them might start to paddle into a swell too small to develop into a wave. I watched these few false starts before the next set of swells appeared, the surfers paddling into position for the new waves. The tide was dropping and a mellow swell was developing, but I stayed up on the Strand to watch Lucas surf. Lucas was an aggressive surfer, and was experimenting with one of the new, shorter boards. The shorter boards made paddling into a wave more difficult, but once in, the shortboards cut and turned and raced sharply and quickly.

I watched Lucas miss a few waves, and suddenly he was up on a thin shoulder. He slashed and dashed across the face of the wave, dropping to his knees as if to pray, and rising, pointed his board like a bayonet and thrust up from the bottom in a long easy cutting curve.

They did not stay in the water long, and as the trio came out I decided to stay where I was on the Strand and say hello to Lucas. I had not talked to him since the reception party at Malone's. Lucas was limping in the soft sand, carefully choosing where to land his feet as he walked up the beach toward the Strand.

"How's the water, Lucas," I yelled, surprising him. "You didn't stay in long."

"Hey, Sal," Lucas said, nodding and smiling. "Just wanted to get wet. Have to go easy on the feet." Lucas put his board down in the sand and got under the outdoor shower below the Strand, and I climbed down to talk to him.

"Have not seen you since the other night, the big party up at Malone's," Lucas said. "Been writing any letters lately?"

"No one to write to," I said.

"Seablouse not over that business about the letters at Malone's yet?"

"No, I don't think so."

"You getting used to civilian life?"

"I don't miss the war."

"But that's too bad, the business about your letters, I mean about Penny freaking out over it. What the hell. Everyone was just having a good time," Lucas said. He had finished his quick rinse in the shower.

"Penina's letters," I said.

"Yeah, well, you said some things I wish I could have said to my girl. Maybe she'd still be my girl."

"You never know."

"That's true," Lucas said. "Yeah, I'm happy to be back in

the surf, but these heels are a bummer."

"You looked good out there today, carving up some waves."

"You going in?" Lucas asked.

"Yes, I was just enjoying watching you on some waves. You like the shortboard?"

"It's hard paddling into the wave. Too much of the board is under water, but once in the wave, the shortboard is radical."

Lucas climbed the steps up from the beach, and I watched him putting his board into the back of his van. I did not know the other two surfers in his trio. The surfers put their boards into the van, laughing in wet trunks and tousling their long hair. They took turns climbing into the van to shed their trunks and pull on jeans. Lucas waved from the van as it rattled off and climbed up the hill.

I walked down to the water, knelt down in the sand and rubbed some fresh wax onto my board. I waded out into the water, slid onto my board, and paddled out. The swells were spinning now like white galvanized pipes threaded with foam, cast iron waves, rope caulked and cold chisel hammered. I took my time picking waves. I was in good physical shape, and I had not lost the feel for the board or the wave. It was now late morning in the middle of a spring week and the water was not crowded. I had a spot at 41st to myself. I caught a fat wave on the shoulder and rode my long board slowly into the inside break where the speed of the wave suddenly picked up and I took a couple of quick steps up to the nose to stay in the curl but then stepped back as the wave closed out ahead, and shifting my weight to the back of the board, I swung the nose around and over the breaking curl, and dropping to my knees, I pushed off the fall of the wave's shoulder and paddled back out to the break.

I stayed in the water for a couple of hours and built an appetite for something to drink and eat. I decided to grab a beer and something to eat at Blubber's, the greasy dive down on the Strand where Penina worked. I did not know if Penina would be there waitressing. I got out of the water and went up to change out of my trunks. I put on a pair of Malone's jeans and one of his "Puck's Boards" tee-shirts and walked back down to the Strand. I followed the Strand to Blubber's, hanging loose in Puck's blousy clothes but feeling solid and good, my skin salted and the hair on my skin stiff from the salt, and I felt happy to be out of uniform and dusted with salt. When I got to Blubber's, I sat down at an outside table on the Strand against the low wall overlooking the beach. Angel Wormth was waitressing the outside tables, and I did not see Penina around.

I drank a tall glass of water and was nursing a beer,

watching the walkers and the waves, when along came Puck riding up the Strand, grinning, playfully pedaling his royal blue bicycle, holding a surfboard under one arm, wiggling to and fro. He was barefoot and shirtless, wearing some baggy trunks. He was watching the waves, closed out, booming bass lines now in the spring high tide. He saw me and parked his bike and leaned his board against the wall.

Puck Malone's neck was as thick as a telephone pole. His face was full and fat, with marble brown eyes spinning between freckled cheeks and straight, sandy-red hair, bowl cut with bangs down to his eyes. His tornado torso funneled down to two skinny legs. He had big surfer knots on his knees and feet from paddling in the kneeling position.

"Hey, man, what's happening?" Malone said, smiling cheerily, pulling a chair up to my table. "Penina here?"

"I've not seen her. Where have you been?"

"This morning I had to go to that meeting down at the business association. I just now grabbed some good waves down south of the pier. Where were you?"

"I watched Lucas Crux carving up some faces with his new shortboard."

"Yeah, Lucas is going to be on the shop's new surf team, I think, as soon as his heels heal. Heelbilly, I call him," Puck said, laughing at himself. "But did you go in?"

"Yes, I was out for a couple of hours."

"I'm stoked to have you back, man."

"Thanks."

"Penina not here this morning?"

"I've not seen her. I thought maybe she was with you."

"You know, don't push it, man. That thing with me and Penina, that was a one time deal, man, I swear, one time, and it wasn't my idea," Malone said. "That's the truth of things." He leaned back, shook his head up and down, back and forth, and looked out over the beach to the water.

"It doesn't matter whose idea it was. Either one of you could have said no."

"Yeah, yeah," Malone said, looking out at the water.

"And what do you do at the end of a wave?" I said.

"Yeah, I know, you paddle back out for another. You know, those damn letters of yours didn't help anything."

"Did Penina think I was not coming back?"

"She prayed every hour of every day for you, man," Malone said, slapping the table with his open hand. "Don't say that. We watched the war on television one night. Then she shows me a couple of these banzai wiped out letters. Next thing I know, she's climbing aboard old Puck. That's the truth of things, man. It was those crazy letters of yours, Salty."

I did not think Puck Malone had ever read a book in his life, but I was not critical of him for that. I rather liked him for it, for Malone was a man of action. He made things, and he could make things happen, and he was seldom bewildered.

"The war was a long time happening, man," Malone said, "a long time. People change. Penina discovered herself while you were away. Maybe some others did too. What the hell, man, you should thank me for keeping that knucklehead Killknot away from her."

A couple of girls in sandals and wearing bathing suits, with towels draped around their shoulders, walked by on the Strand, headed down to the beach, and Puck flirted with them, but they passed without stopping.

"The surfer girls, they come and go," Malone said.

"And the surfers long to know," I said.

"Know what?" Malone said. "That's what I want to know."

"I don't know," I said.

"What the hell," Malone said. "You order something to eat?"

"Yes, bacon and eggs, but I told Angel to take her time with it."

"Angel here? I need a burger and a beer," he said. "I'm going after Angel," he said, and got up to go inside to order.

"So let's see the scar, Salty dog," Malone said, coming back out and sitting down, and I showed him the stitch line that started just below my navel and ran down into my pants. Angel came over from the door with beers and paused to take a look, too. I lowered my pants just enough so they could see where the scar continued on down.

"Oh, Salty," Angel said.

"Sweet Jesus," Malone said. "And they wouldn't send you home with that?"

"It's complicated," I said. "It wasn't that bad, and they don't necessarily send you home. And I didn't want to spend the rest of the war washing floors in some hospital ward."

"How did you do it?" Angel said.

"I rode a boom up to the top of a telephone pole to attach a chain. We were pulling out this line of telephone poles on a remote road."

"Why were you doing that?" Malone said.

"I don't know. Anyway, I slipped and came down on a crossbar."

"Does it hurt?" Angel said.

"No, it's no big deal. I just got cut, and now I have a scar."

"You glad to be home, now, Sal?" Angel said.

"Of course he's glad to be home," Malone said.

"Some soldiers, it's hard on them coming home," Angel said.

"I'm glad to be back," I said. "Looks like the home part might take some work."

"See? That's what I'm talking about," Angel said to Malone.

"He's fine," Malone said. "He just needs to surf and shape, and he'll be fine. Ain't that so, Salty?" Malone said.

"And stay away from loud noises," I said.

"Where's Penina?" Malone asked Angel.

"She had a college class this morning, and she got called in to her grade school to work this afternoon," Angel said. "I'm covering for her because I need all the hours I can get. Baby needs a new pair of shoes," she said, smiling and staring at Malone.

"You have a baby?" I asked.

Angel showed me a picture of a kid a year old already.

"Who's the lucky father?" I asked, but she didn't answer, and she put the picture back in her wallet. I looked at Malone. "Don't look at me," he guffawed. "I ain't nobody's daddy."

Malone gave Angel what I assumed was supposed to be a

playful slap on her bottom and said, "Hey, babe, you coming to the music bar crawl with us? Huh? Come be my date, why don't you?" Malone was now rubbing the back of Angel's thighs.

"Stop that," Angel said, slapping at Malone's arm.

"Ah, now," Malone said. "What happened to 'Oh, Puck, it's so big,' and 'Oh, Puck, it feels so good,' and 'Oh, Puck, don't stop?'" Malone said, laughing and reaching out with his hand for Angel's backside as she pulled away.

"You're disgusting," Angel said, and went back inside.

Puck and I drank the beers she had brought out.

"Yeah, it's good to have you back, man," Malone said.

"It felt good being back in the water," I said.

"It feels clean," Malone said.

"Yes, that's it, Puck. It's the salt."

We drank our beers and watched the water.

Angel brought the bacon and eggs and Malone's burger with a pile of fries out to the table, and we ate. A couple of young surfers walked by with belly boards and fins, and they said hi to Malone.

"Hey," Puck said to the boys, "keep those belly boards inside the flags, huh, guys? Stay out of the way of the surfboards."

"Sure, Puck," one of them said.

"I had to pull some kid out of the water a couple of weeks

ago," Malone said to me, "gash between his eyes, bloody water all down his face and chest. Christ, it's getting too crowded out there. This kid, he duck rolled a wave, and when he came up, he got hit in the face by a loose board. Lucky he didn't pass out and drown."

We went on eating and watching the water. The food was good, and the beer was cold and tasted refreshing after my coming out of the water, sitting in the sun on the Strand with Malone. We watched the two surfer boys put on their fins down by the water and paddle out on their belly boards, letting the white water wash over them as they paddled out through the soup.

I was thinking Malone had embarrassed Angel in front of me and wishing he had not treated her that way and wondering if it would do any good to say something to him about it when I saw her sneaking up behind him with a half pitcher of foamy beer. She must have been swapping out a keg. She put her finger across her lips to signal me not to give her away, and she dashed up and poured the pitcher of beer over Malone's head.

Malone took Angel's beer dousing in stride. "What a waste of good beer," he said, after having let out a yell and turning and seeing Angel running back inside.

"How about taking my bike and board back up to the shop?" he said, wiping his face with a table towel. "I'm going to swim back up to 42nd and walk up from there. Wash this beer off."

"I'm not doing any shaping today," I said. "I'm going into El Segundo to pay my respects to Tom Chippy's folks."

"I'll go with you," Malone said. "I'll see you back at the shop. I won't be long," he said, and he got up and went running across the beach down to the water.

I left some cash on the table for Angel, to cover my and Malone's food and beer, leaving enough for an absurdly big tip. I was on Malone's bike with his board and about to ride away when Angel came back out to clean up.

"See you around," Angel, I said.

"Yeah, Sal," Angel said. "I'm glad you're back all safe and sound and all," she said. She was standing with one arm across her stomach, the elbow of her other arm resting on the hand holding her side, a wet bar towel clutched in her fingers, her other hand held up to catch her falling head with the chin. She looked up into my eyes then looked back down. She had thick black hair tied behind her head in a long ponytail. She was wearing a loose fitting, blue blouse that hung over her wide hips covered with tight, paisley peddle pusher shorts. Puck had reached up under her blouse to feel her bottom. She was standing now her weight on one leg, one foot on top the other. She abruptly broke the pose, combing a loose strand of hair back over her ear.

"I better clean up this mess before Blubber asks about it,"

Angel said. "See you around, Sal," she said.

"Thanks, Angel," I said, and rode off on Malone's bike with his surfboard under my arm, back up the Strand.

I drove my truck with Malone down Vista del Mar and up Grand Avenue into El Segundo. The Chippys lived in one of the old refinery-worker houses just over the sand dunes. We turned off Grand and drove slowly down their street. Through the side yards we could see where the sand had been sliding down the dunes and spilling through twisted, wood slat fences into the back yards. We stopped at Tom's house and climbed out and walked to the front door and knocked.

Mary Chippy, Tom's mother, answered the door, looking distracted, but when she saw who it was, she gasped and threw open the screen door, coming out and grabbing me into her arms, and Tom's dad came to the door to see what all the commotion was about. Mary held my face in her hands and stared into my eyes.

"Look, look who's here, Ray," Mary said, "home from the war."

They invited us in, and Malone and I filled their living room couch. The little couch smelled of lavender, the pillows covered with fresh, ironed linen. The room was clean, and barely

69

looked lived in, not a speck of dust or sand on the hardwood floor, as if they had been expecting guests. Mary sat awkwardly down in her rocker, across from us, pulling her short housedress down over her thighs. She was a narrow, small woman, all elbows and knees and ankles, but with the face of an overripe peach. Her fingers and hands were wrinkled and twisted with arthritis. Her long hair was tied up in a tight, grey bun. Next to her, Tom's dad, Ray Chippy, fell heavily with a sigh into his overstuffed easy chair. He sat with his big hands cupped over the arms of the chair. He wore a buzzcut, and his big, tanned head looked like a bronze sculpture.

Tom's mother said how good I looked, and his dad agreed, and said it looked like the war had done me no harm, but said of course he knew that was probably not true. I started off calling them Mr. and Mrs. Chippy, but they said no. They would feel more comfortable now if we called them by their first names. They asked how Puck was doing, and said they had not seen him since the funeral, but had read an article in a local shopping guide about how his surf shop was getting popular, but it was soon clear they wanted to talk about Tom.

"One night, we was watching the war on the television," Mary said, "and that's how we come to know he'd been hurt."

"I used to watch the war on television every night, every night," Ray said, shaking his head slowly back and forth.

"And then, one night, Suzie yells, 'There's Tom'! In the war, on the television."

"I was sitting right here, and I saw him," Ray said, pounding the arms of his chair, "camera right on his face. You wonder if something like that's gonna happen, if you'll see somebody you know, but you never do, but all of a sudden, wham, there's our Tom."

"They was carrying him on a stretcher, running to a helicopter," Mary said.

"Stooped over, stumbling, weighted down with equipment."

"One of them was holding up the bottle with the tube coming out of it," Mary said, holding her hand over her head to show us.

"You could see the high grass," Ray said, "blowing in the wind under the chopper blades and hear the blades spinning and all kinds a noise, guys yelling."

"Then the camera went back to the news desk. And what could we do but just sit here, like we was knocked out, not knowing what had happened, how bad Tom was hurt."

"We waited for something more," Ray said, "but it was just another night of the war on TV, and as soon as we heard Cronkite saying, 'And that's the way it is,' we turned the TV off and tried to make some phone calls. We got a hold of the Red Cross, and they called us back the next day."

"They tried to save him, but it was too late," Mary said, "too late for Tom." She reached over and touched Ray's hand, but he pulled it away.

"Poor Suzie," Mary said, "she like to faint dead away, all that waiting around for Tom to come home, storing things up for when he got back, playing around in her hope chest, making all kinds of plans, and suddenly see it all come to nothing like that. She used to come over near every night and watch the war on the TV with us."

"Hell, she's already found herself somebody new," Ray said. "But that's the way things should be. I don't fault her none, needing to get on with her life. You know what I mean. What the hell's she gonna do hanging round here, spend all day unfolding and folding his letters?"

"I've saved his letters and his pictures and his flag, but we don't like to display them out," Mary said.

"But I do miss Suzie, too" Ray said. "Don't get me wrong, now."

"I miss them both," Mary said, rubbing her hands together in her lap, rocking quietly back and forth for a few moments.

"I'm sorry Tom didn't make it back," I said, looking first

at Mary then at Ray.

"Grab us some beers, why don't you, Mary?" Ray said, and Mary got up and went into the kitchen.

"The hell of it is, Sal," Ray said, leaning forward and whispering, "is that Tom got hit by what you call that friendly fire, you see. That's the truth of things. That's what got him. Not that it matters, but did you know that, Sal?"

"I don't know. Things did get confused sometimes. But it's hard to say."

"Don't say nothing about that to Mary. It would just open up her bleeding heart all over again." He leaned back in his chair again.

Mary came back into the living room, her arms full with three beers and a Tupperware bowl full of potato chips.

We drank our beers and snacked on the chips.

"Tom, now, he'd of liked some of the jobs I been working lately, up in the canyons. You know what I mean," Ray said.

"Yeah?" I said. "Have you been up in the canyons?"

"Oh, yeah," Ray said. "Up Topanga, I been. Up Malibu. I'm just now on a job, we can see the ocean. I climb up to the roof and eat my lunch and take my shirt off to work off this farmer's tan, you know. Tom used to always kid me about my farmer tan."

"I don't want you climbing up on no more roofs no more,"

Mary said.

"Ah, hell." Ray took a long drink of his beer. "And you can smell the licorice bushes up there, you know what I mean, the air full of the hot canyon smells. And the air so fresh and wet in the morning but by the afternoon all hot and dry. We work until the sun starts to go down, and we drive down to the highway and get us a beer at one of the bars on the water. Yes, Tom would have loved these jobs up in the canyons with me."

We were quiet again, and the room felt smaller. Mary dropped her hand down into a basket of yarn next to her chair and squeezed one of the balls of yarn. Then Ray got up to go into the kitchen, and we knew he was crying. Mary stayed a moment then got up to go into the kitchen.

"Jesus," Malone said.

"Yeah," I said.

An onshore, late afternoon breeze was now coming through the house, drifting down the dune behind the house and coming through the kitchen window, curling through the living room, and passing out the front screen door. We could hear the Chippys whispering in the kitchen. We finished our beers, sitting on the couch in the living room in silence.

Tom's parents came back into the living room. I did not

want to look into their eyes, red and watery, their faces worn and worried looking.

I stood up before they could sit back down and said, "Well, we just wanted to come over and say hi."

"Thank you, boys," Ray said. "Thank you."

Malone got up and said, "Thanks for the beer."

"You boys are welcome here anytime," Mary said, "anytime."

"Tom was a hell of a carpenter," Ray said. "Know that?"

"Yes, sir," I said. "I do know that."

"Why, he could drive 16 penny nails, sinking the heads flat in three swings, leaving no hammer mark, all day long," Ray said.

He reached out and shook my hand, and his hand felt like an open-end wrench, hard but worn smooth. He did not fully open his hand.

We stepped to the front door and went out. We turned to say goodbye to them. They were standing in the open door. Ray went back inside, but Mary walked out to the truck with us.

"Sal," she said, touching my arm. She stopped and looked back at the house.

"I just want to tell you." She paused again, looking into my eyes. "There are no jobs."

"I don't understand," I said. "What jobs?"

"Ray has not been working any jobs in any canyons. Ray has not worked since the day we met Tom's body in his bag coming off the plane from the war."

I looked at Malone. We looked at Mary.

"I just think you boys should know the truth of things," she said.

She stood at the edge of the yard and watched us get into the truck. She took a short step forward and waved and brought her hand to her mouth and covered her lips with her fingers as we drove away.

We did not talk on the way back from Tom Chippy's house to Malone's shop. I parked the truck out front. Malone went to work behind the counter, and I went into the garage and got back to work on a used board I was reshaping. Malone had me stripping the fiberglass off some old, ding damaged longboards and reshaping the foam blanks into shortboards. He had an idea that we should put some big "Puck's Boards" decals on the doors of my truck. He said he would give me some gas money for the advertising. I was living in the shop rent free, but I had told him that arrangement was temporary. I was waiting for Penina. What the hell, Puck had said. I just got back, and I should take my time and take it easy.

I worked in the garage for a couple of hours. I heard Malone locking up the shop, but he did not come in to say goodbye or goodnight. I grabbed some beers and went up to my room above the shop.

Maybe Malone was right and Penina had changed while I was away. She had been working her way through school, and had finished at El Camino, and had now transferred to the new state college out at Dominguez Hills. She had developed aspirations we did not share. I was not interested in going to college. In twelfth grade, going through the motions, I had applied and been accepted to Berkeley, UCLA, and Loyola, but the idea of college had been sucked out of me by the end of high school. Penina had said I had a chip on my shoulder, but that wasn't our problem now. She was working and living on her own, no father, no mother, no family. She had learned to live alone. A soldier might get lonely in the Army, but soldiers do not live alone. Penina wanted a man willing and able to live alone. I had no siblings, but my parents had been socialites, always entertaining, any excuse for a party was their motto, and our home was a hostel for vagrant houseguests. We were always helping someone out. Once, a family of five down on their luck lived with us for six months. My parents when young had aspired to a spurious bohemian lifestyle, but over time my dad

77

had made too much money to afford way-out mores, and in the end, a sudden sea change rose up and blew through the house. My mother's mind failed her, and my father got sick, drowned in alcohol, and our house emptied out, and I decided to skip college and go with the draft, wherever it might take me.

I drank a beer, sitting in an open window in my room above the surf shop. I could see the staggered mess of roofs and crisscrossing wires of the houses below Highland. The air smelled of seaweed. I watched a few cars pass by, entering or leaving the beach cities, watched their red taillights drift off. Maybe some of them were going somewhere, but some were out cruising. Down below the town, the beach was now dark, and in the far distance I could see pieces of the dark line of a burgundy purple horizon. A boat size, red convertible went by loaded with kids, the radio mixing hubbubbly with the road noise and yells from the car. An El Segundo police cruiser drove slowly by and turned down Refugio Street. A few folks were walking to or from the market, probably out for more cigarettes or some forgotten milk or coffee or more beer. I could see the reddish-orange glow of the neon lights down at the Matchbox tavern. A pickup truck stopped, and a couple of longhairs with backpacks and carrying guitar cases hopped out and walked by and turned down Refugio Street. They would probably sleep under one of the lifeguard towers but would be gone by morning. Then the street was quiet, but just as I was thinking the town was turning in for the night, I heard someone shout, followed by the peel of squealing tires and the sound of a bottle breaking on the sidewalk. But just as quickly the silence seemed to return, but behind me, coming over the dunes, I thought I could hear the hum of the oil refinery, but I always heard that sound lately, no matter how far I was from the refinery, as if a conch shell was affixed to my ear.

I thought of walking down to Penina's place to talk to her, but I knew she was probably studying or already sleeping. She had told me she had an early schedule for the week, and while she would not have turned me away, she would not have appreciated my spoiling her peace. She had told me she was feeling peaceful now that I was back and the letters had stopped coming. She was feeling mellow and peaceful knowing I was near and out of harm's way, she said. She said she hadn't realized how much energy she had burned worrying about me. Now that I was back, she suddenly felt lighter and free and easy. And she said she had read my new letter and had walked down to the jetty and thrown the letter into the water, to save me the trouble, but I did not believe that, for she said she was not going to discourage any new letters. She told me to keep writing.

So I sat down at my desk and wrote her another new letter.

I felt a writer's block as I tried to get going on this one. Most of what I had to tell her she no doubt already knew, but I didn't feel like conjuring up any more love letters. I needed something new to persuade Penina to hook up her shelter half with mine. Here is that second letter:

Dear Penina,

Puck and I drove over to say hi to Tom Chippy's folks late this afternoon. I wanted to pay his parents a visit, and I did not want to wait too long. I ate many late morning breakfasts in Mary Chippy's kitchen after coming out of the water with Tom and Malone. Some summer days, a swarm of hungry surfers would pile out of a van and into their small house, and Tom's mother would scramble up a dozen eggs mixed with green peppers, and toast a loaf of bread, and boil a pot of oatmeal with bananas, and we would eat it all and drink a gallon of milk and another of orange juice.

Mr. Chippy talked about some jobs he's been working on up in the canyons and how Tom would have loved being up there with him, working as a carpenter, out in the open, working in the heat of the canyons. They take their shirts off in the afternoons, Mr. Chippy said. But as we were leaving, Mrs. Chippy told us Ray has not been working any jobs. But I know Tom would have liked working up there with his father in the canyons with his shirt off, his tool belt slung low, the handle of his hammer well worn, the palms of his hands calloused, the backs of his hands sunburned brown. It's a lucky man who knows what he wants and how to get it and how to handle it once he's got it, and it's lucky too for his friends and family if what he wants is simple and hardworking and honest and productive. Mr. Chippy's hands are cupped half-closed from a lifetime of gripping the handles of tools, and he can no longer open his hands fully. There are worse signs of a worker's life, of wear and tear, my father's diseased liver, for example. Surfing is simple, hardworking, in a way, and honest, but I admit it's not productive, and there's certainly no money in it, not for me, anyway, and Malone makes as much selling clothes and accessories out of his shop as he does selling surfboards, and anyway, what he really wants to do is develop property. But you know this.

But writing helps me make sense of things. And some ideas, if you don't sit down to write, may never come to visit. So I'm keeping a journal, some of which I'll share with you, if you feel like reading my mind. I'm thinking of turning my new letters to you into a book. What do you think of that idea? Books would not be as easy as letters to destroy. And even if someone did throw your book away, there would be other copies, on shelves everywhere, in libraries and bookstores, and on tables set up at flea markets and swap meets, and in knapsacks, and sticking out of back pockets and out of purses, and in churches and schools and waiting rooms and convalescent homes, in jails and in penthouses, and in book stalls at the airport and train station and bus station, on the road in cars and in motels and hotels and campgrounds and corner markets, and in sidewalk newsstands, and on the dash board of taxi cabs, and on a towel beneath an umbrella at the beach, in bicycle baskets, and in coffee houses, and in newspaper drives, and in homes, in bedrooms and kitchens and living rooms. Everywhere you looked, everywhere people go, you'd be able to find a copy of *Penina's Letters*.

Henry Killknot knows what he wants, though what Henry wants may not be good for him. It's funny how often what we want is bad for us. Malone knows what he wants, and he's not afraid to take risks. He's in a good place to take advantage of his knowledge and skills, and he's building assets. Malone learned a few things about business talking to my dad. That's where Puck decided he wanted to work for himself. Dad helped Puck write his first business plan. Guys like Lucas and Humulus are as fickle as a woman's hairstyle or fingernail polish or appetite for men. But it doesn't much matter anymore what Hoppy wants, as long as Mary Humulus wants it first. But whatever Lucas and Hops end up doing, they'll make it what they want. They have the ability to find interest in just about anything. They are not easily bored. I think it must be a skill keeping oneself entertained by intrinsically boring tasks. But Lucas says Hoppy is drinking himself silly. Hard to picture John Humulus already married with two kids, drinking himself wacky. His deferments have caught up with him. But the biggest surprise so far is Henry Killknot, a lawyer in a plush office, driving a fancy red sports car, wing tipped toes light on the pedals. I have not seen Peggy Ann since the party.

I saw Angel Wormth today. You probably already know this, too. Malone and I drank some beer, and I polished off a plate of bacon and eggs and toast while Malone demolished a deluxe king-size burger, down at Blubber's. I hadn't seen Angel yet. She missed the party because she couldn't find a sitter for her daughter. I didn't even know she had a child. Puck was rude to Angel. He slapped her on her butt, Malone style, playing around, and Angel would have shrugged him off, but I think she was embarrassed that I saw Puck harassing her, and later she snuck back out (we were sitting at one of the outdoor tables set up on the Strand) and dumped a half pitcher of beer over his head. But why did you never tell me about Angel, a waitress with a child with no father?

Malone was talking about a cruise through the beach cities some Saturday night soon. He said he keeps running into guys still asking about me, and we'd see some of them in a bar crawl, and it wouldn't seem like old times until we've been up and down the beaches a few times good and drunk. Did we used to do that? Sometimes I think we invent or exaggerate old times to justify some new or deepened want. Anyway, I told him I wasn't interested in the old times anymore, and I think he was actually offended. He wants to start this club crawl off at the Matchbook and make our way down to the Lighthouse, stopping at bars and clubs along the way. I'm not sure I like going into bars. Bars can be interesting places though, like boxes, live theatre, good places to hear the different ways people talk. Malone says your folk songs are going to surprise the daylights out of me. That's what he said. I didn't realize you were so serious about your folk act. Will you sing "When Johnny Comes Marching Home" for me? How about "Cruel War?"

Seems like I've not had a chance to really talk to you my first week back, except all that nonsense about your letters. Maybe you're actually glad I tossed the letters, and Penina's Pout is all an act, a fancy decoy to avoid seeing me. But come with me on Malone's club crawl or bar walk or whatever it is, and I'll come listen to your songs. Maybe later you'll let me come home with you, and we'll sit out on your deck, and you can do your homework while I write you a letter, and we'll fall back on the couch and fall asleep outside watching the stars and listening to the surf, the air cool and salty floating over us. I want to smell you and taste the salt on your skin and breathe in your breath and smell that bubblegum scented shampoo you use in your hair. I'll give you a foot rub, no strings attached. You know you'd like that after a week of working tables and tending bar at Blubber's.

Remember the time you arranged for your dad to visit you at my folks' house? He arrived drunk in a taxi. Later, you told me about how after your parents divorced, and you would stay with him for a night or two, he used to leave you in the car while he went into a bar for a beer. And you said I reminded you of the way your dad used to smell. Anyway, I wrote a little poem for you, thinking of you and your dad and how he used to leave you all alone in the car when you were a little girl while he went into a bar for a beer. Here's the poem, but it doesn't have a title:

Her dad drops into a bar to wet his whistle with beer.
Penina waits in the big car, on her cheek, a salty tear.
"I won't last last, my lass," he laughs.
"Take the helm and give it a little gas."

Alone at the wheel she watches the bar door swing free.
She falls asleep while he flirts and stills the floozy ones.

Smelling of smoke and beer, he slams the door, pulls the choke.

She tastes a touch of joy, a wet kiss, a small toy, a pink umbrella.

The beer has made him warm in a way she could not.

And she meets a perfumed Bella, her father's friend.

She spends the night in the front seat of the car, in a parking lot,

while her dad explains to Bella what to do with a drunken sailor.

I'm beat tonight, but I don't feel like bed. I'm going to put this letter in an envelope and walk down and slip it under your door. If I find Malone there, I'm going to grab his surfboard and paddle out to sea and turn into a sea monster who haunts the beaches of the South Bay, spouting and spraying poems up the beaches that only you will be able to read. But I hope you like your poem. You can sing it from the rooftops of Refugio, and I promise I will never throw it into the water.

Love, Sal

~ ~ ~

Henry Killknot

After a couple of nights sleeping head to toe with Penina, and another sleeping out on the deck, and another down on the beach under the lifeguard tower at 42nd Street, I had decided to bunk up at Puck Malone's ramshackle beach house, in an empty room above the surf shop. I kept busy, surfing mornings and shaping new boards in the afternoons, and the next time I saw Penina, she and Henry Killknot came chummily waltzing into the surf shop on roller skates. Henry had lost none of his affected mannerisms. He had always wanted to be an actor, but had sublimated that desire by becoming a lawyer.

"What's with the roller skates?" I said.

"Roller skates are becoming all the new rage," Henry said. "Where's Puck Malone, sole proprietor? I have a business proposition for the astute entrepreneur. We think he should start renting these roller skates out of his shop."

"What are you doing running around with this kook?" I asked Penina.

"Lovely party the other night," Henry said. "And welcome back our Odysseus, well known for his military prowess," he said, rolling over to me, arms open for a hug, but losing his balance, feet rolling forward ahead of his legs, arms flailing, he fell backwards to the floor, landing squat on his butt.

"Ouch," Henry said, climbing back to his feet. "If Malone does start renting these crazy shoes, he'd better get disclaimers and waivers and renter beware notices signed."

"It's not funny," Henry said to Penina, whose healthful laugh I was glad to hear.

"We've come to rescue you from this toilful place," Henry said, back on his feet and rolling again clumsily around the shop. "Come, good friend and unbridled correspondent, and go roller skating with us, down to the Strand, where we shall debut our new sporting habit and be known up and down the beach as true trendsetters."

"Who talks like that?" I said.

"Did you forget? He does," Penina said.

"Where's Malone?" Henry said.

"He's trying to work out a deal to open another store on the Venice Boardwalk," I said.

"Ah, the capitalist pig," Henry said. "Close up, Sally," Henry said, "and let's go skating."

"Puck's probably close to coming back now," I said. "He's been gone all day."

"I think I'm finished skating for now," Penina said, and

rolling over to a chair, sat down to take off her skates.

"I shall sally solo and leave you here solo with Sally, then, my lovely and tender letter fodder, Penina," Henry said.

"Don't fall again," Penina said. "You're going to hurt yourself."

"My butt is a breadbox, my heart a mailbox. My butt rises from the floor, but my mailbox is empty. Do you think Salvador here will write me a letter?"

"If he does, you better make a copy and hide it away," Penina said.

"Yes, Persequi. Who authorized you to throw away Penina dear's dear letters? You concupiscent cad."

"Who authorized you to bring up the subject of the letters, traitor?" I said.

"I've no reason to commit treason, nor am I a collaborationist. I wear but one coat, right side out. Penina will not ride with me? Sally will not ride? I go forth solo, as I said, alone, the number one emblazoned on my escutcheon," Henry said, and he rolled unsteadily out of Puck's shop.

Henry Killknot and I had been classmates together at the Catholic high school in Venice. He was a senior when I was a freshman, but we became acquainted through a mentor program that paired senior boys with freshman boys to help the latter through their first year. The mentor program ostensibly helped the seniors too, since it gave them a chance to develop and practice some leadership skills. St. Gelda was a college preparatory school (the closest thing the school had to a shop class was mechanical drawing), and after graduating, Henry went on to UCLA in the ROTC program and later attended the UCLA law school. We remained friends, thanks to our shared interest in surfing and his interest in mentoring, but it was clear from the beginning of our relationship that I was a disappointing protégé. Henry insisted we follow the procedure of the mentor program, so I had to meet with him daily for the first month, and weekly thereafter. These meetings would consist of a question and answer period, Henry providing both the questions and the answers. Henry was a fine surfer, and he invited me to join his set, which surfed primarily El Porto waters, which is how I met Puck Malone, and it was Malone who had introduced me to Penina. But Henry pestered me with his question and answer drills even after he had moved on to UCLA. Occasionally, he would stop by my house in Playa del Rey after a surf session, using his defunct mentor status as a pretense for bumming something to eat, and one day, for example, he dropped by, let himself in through the garage door, and barged into my room.

"What are you reading there, Persequi," Henry asked me, immediately reclaiming his mentor role, seeing the paperback I had tossed near my satchel on the bed.

"Oh, nothing, just a book," I said.

"Hand it over, Sally," he ordered, and I reluctantly got up and gave him my copy of Jerzy Kosinki's "The Painted Bird."

"I asked you not to call me that," I said.

"Ah, feeling salty are we today?" Henry said.

"I'm familiar with this book," Henry said, "and you should not be reading it," and he stuck it in his back pocket, expecting me, no doubt, to try to grab it back from him, but I simply shrugged him off.

Undeterred, Henry then proceeded to tell me what I should be reading. "Have you ever heard of a little book titled 'Mr. Blue' by Myles Connolly?"

"Yes, we read it last year in Mr. Ford's English class."

"Well, you should read it again. Read it once a year. That's how you treat classics. Read them once a year. You should not be reading this crap Kosinski spews out."

"Have you read 'The Painted Bird'?" I asked.

"No," he said, pulling it back out of his pocket and tossing it onto my desk. "I've been re-reading 'Mr. Blue.' You should consider falling in love with Our Lady, as Blue did, devoting your life to a worthy cause. This Kosinski fellow is a hack."

"But you haven't read him," I said.

"I've tasted him and found him not to my liking, not up to my ethical standards."

"That's nonsense," I said. "Why should Kosinski care about your sense of ethics?

"Doesn't matter. My point now is that you should re-read classics. Stick with them, until you've got things right. Did you not like 'Mr. Blue'?"

"Yes, I liked it well enough."

"Then why are you reading this Kosinski crap? Do you imagine they are true, these wartime atrocities the little boy experiences?"

"What difference would it make? Is 'Mr. Blue' true?"

"There's a difference between fiction and non-fiction. In any case, Mr. Blue was true to Our Lady."

"Jesus, Henry, give me a break."

"I will give you a break, just long enough to steal down to your well-larded pantry and make me a sandwich of ham on softly toasted rye with mustard, mayonnaise, and relish. Toast the bread, but don't burn it. And pour me a tall glass of milk, too, please."

I went down to the kitchen to fetch his lunch while he took over my bed and thumbed through the Kosinski. When I came back up loaded down with plate and tall glass of milk, he said he had immediately had to drop off looking at the Kosinski for fear of losing his appetite. He was now thumbing through one of my dad's *Playboy* magazines he had found in my room.

"Ah," he said, "Now here's something that'll grow the appetite. How's your father doing?"

"Not good. He's lost hope, but he is back working part time."

"I'm sorry to hear that. But let me get to work on that sandwich. Plenty of ham in there. Good man, Private Persequi. Are you going to homecoming prom?" he asked, his mouth full of ham and rye.

"I think so."

"What courtly lady have you asked?"

"Penina Seablouse."

"Never heard of her," he said. "What kind of crazy name is that?" he asked, wiping a glob of mayo across his lips, talking with his mouth full of sandwich.

"She goes to public school, El Segundo," I said.

"She a Catholic?"

"She doesn't go to church."

"Why not? She a communist?"

"She lives alone with her mom. Her parents are divorced."

"And this is the kind of girl you propose to take to Saint Gelda's homecoming prom, a bastard girl from a broken home in a refinery town? And is her mother a waitress in a bar in Hawthorne? Have you already asked her?"

"Sort of."

"What do you mean, sort of?"

"I wrote her a letter, but I've not received a response yet."

"You wrote the daughter of a harlequin strumpet a letter asking the hussy to go to the prom with you?"

"Yes. I wrote her a letter," I said. "Not that it matters, but weren't harlequins males?"

"You're practically hopeless, Sal, but I'm not giving up on you. It's my duty as your mentor to turn you into a worthy adversary. Have you a picture of her?"

"Yes."

"Show."

I took Penina's freshman class picture from my wallet and gave it to Henry. He now had a yellowish mayonnaise squeezing from the corners of his mouth and dripping down his chin.

"Not bad, not bad," Henry said, staring at Penina's photo. "At least she looks like a surfer girl. Peroxide blond hair, bangs. Nice chubby cheeks. Blue eyes. Coy smile. I approve of her looks, anyway," and he let out a loud burp.

"What's her father do?" Henry asked.

"Apparently he drinks for a living."

"So he's in sales. I've heard that's actually a popular job."

"My dad thought so."

"What are you going to be when you grow up, Salty?"

"A writer."

"Where did you get that foolish idea?"

"My mom, I guess."

"A young man should honor his mother but emulate his father."

"My mother is put away, and my father is an alcoholic on his last legs. Some architect. He thinks less is more is a preference for whiskey neat over beer."

"Just remember, Salvador, when you feel like criticizing your parents, not everyone has had the advantages you've had."

"Have you been reading Gatsby again?"

"Very good. Too bad they don't pay people to read. You'd get rich fast."

"I don't care about riches."

"That's easy for you to say. You've got some."

"What about surfing for a living?"

"The beauty of surfing is that it costs little and pays nothing. It cannot be adulterated," Henry said.

"I might have to remember that."

"Don't forget to credit your mentor."

Lieutenant Henry Killknot had finished law school and passed the Bar exam while satisfying his military obligation as a reserve in the National Guard, and he was still in the Guard when I got back from my active duty stint. Henry fancied himself a military aficionado yet had effectively avoided going to war, but I did not hold that against him, and was glad we had not been in combat together, for I would have regretted having to shoot him.

Henry had military orders confused with Holy Orders. He thought of officers as priests and enlisted men as acolytes. The idea had replaced his collapsed church. There were no women in his Guard unit, but had there been, he would have considered them subservient nuns. But Henry was a hard read, even for me, who knew him well. He had entered high school thinking that some day he might want to become a priest, but he was soon disabused of that idea, and the change in him suggested what could happen when traditions are cut loose and drift away from their moorings. His father was habitually out of work, an unskilled laborer, a tinker, the nuns called him, and Henry was the oldest of nine children. They lived in a low rent neighborhood in Venice, and Henry struggled at Gelda with things like being unable to afford the wing tip shoes popular with the boys. His tuition was paid by a scholarship funded by the Knights of Columbus. For a time, surfing distracted Henry from ideas having to do with the importance of wing tip shoes, but Gelda was a place where a boy's father's occupation follows him like a lisp, and while Henry spoke clearly enough, he felt stigmatized because his father officially had no occupation. Henry sometimes said his dad was a fisherman, but the story did not hold water. Henry's dad had been spotted more than once going through trash cans down along the Venice Boardwalk. And Henry was horrified and humiliated that his father was hard of hearing and spoke with a debilitating stutter.

There had been a waiting list of over 400 names when Henry presented himself to the First Sergeant of his local Guard unit. The Sergeant had asked Henry only one question: what did his father do for a living? The question took Henry by surprise, and he said his father was a plumber. Henry had wanted to answer something with some respectability, but did not want to stray too far from the truth, and apparently on the strength of that answer, First Sergeant Bulldorf had taken Henry in, ahead of the 400 plus others. Henry never did understand Bulldorf's selection process, but Henry's ROTC experience had not seemed to make a difference to Bulldorf. Henry went home and asked his father if he indeed had ever done any plumbing work, to measure the extent to which he had lied to Bulldorf, and his dad told of a time he had been hired to clean up a collapsed cesspool, but he soon quit the job because of an itchy rash that had developed on his hands and was growing up his arms.

"What kind of job is that?" Henry had asked me. He had again stopped by my house, to tell me the story of his joining the Guard. "What do you call someone who repairs cesspools?" he said. "I'm the son of a botcher," he said.

"I don't know," I said. "Forget about it."

"I can't forget about it," Henry said. "He's my father, for Christ's sake, and he follows me wherever I go. Father's occupation? Muffer, muffing muckup."

"Jesus said it doesn't matter who your father is," I said, "where you come from, all that crap you get so worked up about."

"Beautiful," Henry said. "If I didn't feel so beat to crap right now, I'd beat the hell out of you for coming up with that," Henry said.

Henry liked to argue, and someone told him he should become a lawyer, and he was flattered by the idea and worked a couple of summer internships at a Westwood law office, where he learned that a good way to prepare for law school was to become an English major and study rhetoric, and when I got back from the war, he was already ensconced in a successful law office on

Wilshire Boulevard's Miracle Mile, which he drove to from a bachelor pad in Refugio in a candy apple red sports car. The office carpets were so deep and plush he was having trouble wearing out a pair of his wing tip shoes, yet he had purchased a fleet of them.

But I doubted that Henry would succeed at law. Some men do not feel complete without an opponent. They are always looking for an argument. They have a chip on their shoulder, but only one chip. They are unbalanced. Something is always bothering them, and they cannot feel whole without getting someone into the ring with them. Given the opportunity, this type of man might go to law school and become a lawyer, and so never does outgrow the need everywhere he goes to feel around for a foe to complete his picture of himself. The opponent man thinks in terms of opposites, but paradoxically, what he wants is to get into the ring with a man like himself, another opponent man. It is no good being matched up with an ambivalent man, for the doubtful cannot be worthy opponents, and create awkward, unsymmetrical pictures. Thus the opponent man is doomed to frustration, for the picture of two opponent men coupled in a ring can never be a whole one. It will always be lopsided. Such was the case with Henry Killknot.

Henry thought he would be a successful lawyer because he saw himself as coming from the ranks of the opponent men, worthy adversaries all, but what he learned was that the most effective lawyers are opportune men, two-faced emotional bluffs, who can argue either side of an argument equally persuasively, and do not much care which side they argue, and care not for the win, or for justice, for rights or wrongs, but for the money, and when the money piles up to the right height, a deal is cut. Whether or not any of this discussion about lawyers is accurate or true in general does not matter, because Henry came to believe it, and so he witnessed his second, after the church, life buoy sinking. And he started to talk about what a man is, his essence, as only of interest with respect to what he thinks he is, his essence rarely connected to his occupation, which is usually a matter of chance. Henry Killknot was too conflicted to be a productive lawyer. Efficient lawyers value compromise, and Killknot was not prepared to compromise his pride, yet he now thought life was a burlesque, and he loved the show, and his lampooning effectively masked the shame he felt at being the son of a stuttering day laborer.

I thought Henry and Malone might have conspired on the caper of Penina's letters. Henry would have been the idea man and Malone the secret agent in Henry's Operation Envelope espionage fantasy. Malone was Penina's landlord, and had a key to her place. Henry would have egged Malone on, mixing the idea into the welcome home reception work as if planning for a bachelor party, Penina to pop out of a cake. Malone was a prankster, laughingly going along with the idea, Henry a bad hat, deceptive and devious motives growing like burls out of what started as a practical joke.

Henry was a bitter young man who held grudges and provoked fights, yet he still suffered from hyper-enthusiasms, which would leave him feeling deflated, unmoored, and greatly disappointed. He was an actor, and effectively masked his disappointments with his affected personality quirks. His first great disappointment came from his having wanted to become a priest. The club would have him, but first he had to understand the terms on which he was to be accepted. But Henry was not helpless, and the son of the ignoble day laborer was quick to wrestle away from the foolishness of the club's rules. Still, he remained disappointed that the club was not what he had thought it to be.

Henry's coming of age was pockmarked with a spreading emotional acne of popped bubbles. High school for Henry was a painful peeling away of naïve but deep assumptions about how the world's business is negotiated. His own high school anecdotes, which he enjoyed repeating to innocent ears, illustrated the miseducation and maledictions of Henry Killknot. Though there was nothing in his experience amounting to acute trauma, the pile of all the tiny insults and humorous humiliations was a dam of crap that needed flushing away.

Henry liked to remind me of his Holy Ghost story. I think Henry still believed in grace as a gift from God, but he failed to see that God's gifts are often practical jokes. Pigeons and seagulls frequently collected in the breezeway between the building wings at Gelda, which was near the beach in Venice. One day, Henry caught a pigeon and let it loose in Father Trip's religion class. "It's the Holy Ghost, Father!" Henry exclaimed. Who knows, maybe it was, for all the fire that followed. Henry got suspended for a few days. When he came back, I heard he had fallen asleep in Mr. Q's senior civics class. I asked him about it. He laughed and said he had heard a little slap. He slowly lifted his head, drooling onto his desk. There stood Mr. Q, his small, scattergun paddle in his hand. The seats were empty, the class at the front of the room, in the doorway, watching. Mr. Q had just hammered his paddle down on the desk in front of Henry, thinking no doubt Henry would jump and it would make for a good laugh and lesson. Henry looked up at Q. "I must have fallen asleep," Henry said. Q's look softened. "Come on, Dad," he said, "class is over; time to move out." Henry had not forgotten Mr. Q for what he considered was an act of kindness. Henry was so tired because he had been waking up before four every morning to deliver a pickup truck load of Los Angeles Times newspapers before school, a job he shared for a time with his father.

But is kindness a lightening of cruelty? "They're a bunch of Morlocks," Henry said, referring to the faculty. We'd been introduced to the Morlocks when we read H. G. Wells's "The Time Machine" in freshman English class. At the end of each class, the Morlocks had to stand next to their desks while Mr. Sandjob dismissed them row by Morlock row. "Jesus," Henry said, "that's funny," when I told him about Sandjob's procedure. "Yes," I said, "but don't you see, they've introduced us to the Morlocks; they've introduced us to themselves. Why would they do that?" Henry had no answer. "Sandjob lines us up and calls us Morlocks," I said. "But we aren't the Morlocks. We're the Eloi. They are the Morlocks."

"I'm going to talk to Sandjob for you," Henry said, looking like he had just been struck with an epiphany. Later, Henry would not tell me what he had said to Sandjob, but whatever he said, he was awarded another day of suspension to his record.

The closest offering to a skilled-worker prep-class at the school was the mechanical drawing class. Henry and I both wanted to take the class, and, since there was only one class, they mixed the grades, so we took the class together. Alas, we got Mr. Ralpher, a football coach who knew nothing about mechanical drawing. Early in the year, every Monday, during class time, we watched football films from the previous Friday night's game. One day, Henry came to class wearing Glen plaid slacks, square patterned, checkered pants. They were hand-me-downs from an uncle's second hand suits. But Ralpher took the pants for a rebel without a cause statement, a counter-culture comment, and Ralpher made Henry come to the front of the room, climb up on the elevated teacher's desk, and model the pants for the class. Ralpher probably also thought the pants suggested an effeminate inclination. Henry had to turn around in a circle on Ralpher's desk three times, with his arms spread horizontally. I looked up at Henry and smiled, an empathetic, don't let it bother you smile. Ralpher was watching him with a leering smile. And I learned that Henry had a dangerous romantic tendency, and I also realized how desperate he was to escape his predicament. He thought he could teach Mr. Ralpher a lesson. Henry leaped from the desk and landed on Ralpher, taking him to the floor. But Ralpher, a footballer and a wrestler, quickly subdued Henry. At the time, we all thought it was to Ralpher's credit that he did not report the incident, for which Henry would have been expelled. But maybe Henry would have been better off expelled. He might still have had some chance at an ordinary life, and I later questioned what might have been in Ralpher subversive motives. He could have had Henry expelled, but it might have been more useful to keep Henry around.

Henry had a remarkable memory. I think he probably had a photographic memory. For Sandjob's class, my buddy Mix and I would, in the hall just before class, memorize a quick, short poem, something by Frost, for example, recite it to one another to make sure we had it, and go in and recite it for Sandjob to score some quick extra credit points. We would usually forget the poem as quickly as we had memorized it. One day, hearing Mix and me in the hall getting a quick poem down, Henry scoffed at us and proceeded to recite by heart T. S. Eliot's "The Waste Land."

"Why are you wasting your time on those little poems," Henry said, "when you could score in a single shot a surplus of points that would carry you through to the end of the term?"

"What does it all mean?" Mix said.

"What does what mean?" Henry said.

"Any of it," Mix said, "this Wasteland and Prufrock business."

"If you can't see the cat in the fog," Henry said, "you might want to forget about poetry. Prufrock is frocked and fogged, pettifogged," Henry said. "He's just a figure of speech."

"I hate poetry," Mix said, as Henry sauntered off down the hall.

I had always had mixed feelings about Henry. My locker was in the connecting hall above the breezeway. I avoided going to it if Henry was around. His locker was next to mine. I found him intimidating, and he was prone to pranks. But Henry graduated, and while I had disliked his mentoring, I came to appreciate that Henry had four years on me and was willing to share his experiences from a critical and analytical perspective. Not that I followed him. It was in part under Henry's influence that I decided to go the active duty route and not even try to get into the Guard, where I might have avoided going overseas and having to become a real soldier tied up in the war. Yet I liked Henry for what I considered his hard-earned, hard-boiled cynicism. And I liked that he took reading seriously. He and I both believed that books offered a salvation we did not see anywhere else, outside the surf. We were not so naïve that we thought writers were saints, though some were certainly saintlier than others, Dorothy Day, Simone Weil, and Henry Miller, who Henry Killknot considered a true priest. Yet Henry was cynical even of books, and does an overdose of cynicism turn us all into Morlocks, cannibalizing the last soft parts of human nature?

When I was a senior, my Dad bought me what later the locals called Penina's Peace Truck. One day, walking through the parking lot, I noticed that every car had a book sitting on the windshield. I got to my truck, wondering what the book could be. It was "Masters of Deceit," by J. Edgar Hoover. We had bought the truck from Les Rotare, who was leaving for the war. Lester was one of the first soldiers we knew personally who got sent home in a body bag. I mentioned the Hoover book to Henry the next time I saw him. "Morlocks," was all Henry would say, shaking his head.

Corporal punishment, in the form of wood paddle spankings, was prevalent at the school, and I remember a time when Mr. Branch had given Henry some swats. Branch had just built a new paddle out of a piece of plywood, painted bright red, with holes drilled into it, a large rectangle affixed to a short handle. The girls were outside, in their separate lunch period, and a few of them had watched the swats through the classroom windows. Later, one of them, Judy, a friend of mine, told me Henry had cried. It seemed unlikely she could have noticed that through the window, even if Henry had cried, so I did not know if she had wanted him to cry, or had not wanted him to cry, if she was sorry for the swat, or disappointed Henry had not withstood it better, was being sympathetic, or was making fun of Henry. No one ever swatted the girls, that I knew of, and it was hard to know what the girls thought about the swat business that went on in the boys' classes.

When you know a guy through his coming of age years like I knew Henry Killknot, you might feel that you understand him somewhat, his motivations, his angers, his loves, his fears, but guys that age can turn quickly, and they probably do not yet know themselves, how they will react to unforeseen situations and events, so how could someone else know them? The child is not father to the man. Most men do not remember Wordsworth's child, and while they might spend an inordinate amount of time at a certain place in their life looking for him, they come to feel at last that one must get rid of any thought of the other if there is ever to be peace. Henry had entered high school wanting to cash in on an advantage he had been given, and he left an angry young man, believing the father had ruined the child.

It was not until he got to UCLA that Henry discovered dope, in spite of, or maybe because of, his ROTC status. The dope seemed to do him some good, sweetening his moods. But then he discovered law, and desperately shaking the dirt from his blue collar, determined he would get rich bringing to the surface and suing into light all the Morlocks he could get his hands on. His taste for dope turned into yet another false fix that for Henry quickly turned sour. I remained ambivalent toward Henry. He was often unpleasant to be around, but I liked him because I thought I understood him, and, thinking I understood him, I made the mistake of feeling an affinity for him, and of feeling sorry for him.

I was thinking Henry must have had something to do with the pinching of Penina's letters as I sat down to write her a third, new letter. Puck Malone was not a reader, Henry was. Then another thought rose to the surface, like a dead fish. Henry was a hoarder, a collector. He saved everything. He was a baseball card collector, and hoarded even the most obscure players. He collected stamps and coins. He had a collection of tattered postcards written by soldiers in previous wars. He had saved all the papers he had ever written for school. He had written me monthly letters when I was away, and he had made and saved copies of them for his own files, as he called them, with copies of my replies. They would be valuable some day, Henry said, though he did not explain why.

And Henry was a reader who respected books. He had built up a sizable personal library, and he still owned the cheap paperback copies of books he had read in high school, cheap Signet Classics: Poe's "The Fall of the House of Usher and Other Tales"; Melville's "The Confidence Man"; "The Time Machine"; "Notes from Underground." I do not know if he continued to read them, but he would never toss them. He was a romantic and sentimental. He was romantic and sentimental about the military, and he was sentimental about his books, no matter how unsentimental the stories those books might tell. He was a great fan of nostalgic war movies. My letters to Penina would never be part of the literary canon, but Henry Killknot knew Penina cared not for the canon, but for her letters. Penina's letters might give Henry Killknot two opportunities, one of which might satisfy some nefarious purpose. They might simply make a nice addition to his personal collection of obscure marginalia and memorabilia, which he was already absurdly planning to will to the library at UCLA, or he might use them as leverage against Penina or me. Perhaps he was entertaining some scheme of coercion.

My suspicions about the purloined letters turned away from Malone to Henry. But if Henry Killknot did have something to do with stealing the letters, would he have let them be destroyed? Probably not, if he could somehow save them. Did Henry still have some or all of Penina's letters? Is so, what had I thrown off the Refugio jetty? And why would Henry be keeping the letters?

These questions occupied me as I wrote Penina's next letter:

Dear Penina,

I spent the weekend on assignment as an official, special correspondent with Henry Killknot's Guard unit. I mentioned this idea to you when I first got home. I had hoped to take notes as an independent observer of the weekend drill, interviewing some of Henry's platoon members, and write something to submit freelance to one of the local papers. I was looking forward to the opportunity of writing something with a sincere purpose for an actual audience.

Can you please read what I've drafted so far and comment? I'll give it to you here, beginning with my title:

"National Guard Drills On Backlot"
By Salvador Persequi, Independent Reporter

Culver City, CA – Area National Guard units converged for their monthly training exercise at an MGM studio backlot last weekend. The units deployed to the studio in Army troop carriers. The giant green trucks convoyed off the freeway and rumbled through local city streets before disappearing behind the backlot walls.

Lieutenant Henry Killknot, a recent graduate from UCLA's law school and an ROTC veteran, took the training seriously, leading his platoon through a weekend of riot control exercises.

"You never know when the drill will get real," Lt. Killknot

said.

The National Guard has partnered with local police agencies to coordinate planning, preparation, and training for control of possible future events of civil unrest. The MGM backlot in Culver City was secured as a training site for its make believe possibilities.

Some of the troops volunteered to act as "aggressors" during the drill. The studio backlot, with its narrow streets lined with staged fronts and scalfolded building backs, offered an ideal setting for the troops to experience the chaos that can quickly unfold in an uncontrolled urban environment.

During the riot control exercise, Lieutenant Killknot's platoon received orders to subdue several aggressors who had set up mock barricades on New York Avenue. The aggressors were clearly enjoying their chance to act out the attitudes often associated with today's protest generation.

The platoon moved slowly forward. The aggressors threw rubber rocks and plastic bottles, and soldiers ducked into doorways for cover.

One of the aggressors, costumed in disheveled clothing, ran forward, dancing crazily in the street, taunting Lt. Killknot's men.

"Hold your ground," Henry Killknot shouted to his

platoon. No one moved.

Killknot's Bridge Platoon is part of an Engineer company. While professionally trained for combat missions or disaster relief, they have little civil disorder experience. They have been drilled this weekend to recognize that civil unrest agitators are not an enemy.

But the aggressor crossed the barricades and ran amok into the platoon's position.

Lt. Killknot ordered Specialists Eugene Cumbers and August Wormth to apprehend the aggressor.

Cumbers and Wormth took hold of the aggressor and handed him off to an infantryman who escorted him away from the dysfunctional zone to an aggressor holding tank where he was questioned and arrested for disorderly conduct. The action was all part of the simulated drill.

Lt. Henry Killknot's platoon quickly vanquished the aggressors and liberated New York Avenue.

"We'll continue to train to prepare for a variety of contingencies," Lt. Killknot said.

The troops exited the studio backlot late Sunday afternoon, and things returned to normal on New York Avenue.

Signed: Salvador Persequi, reporting from the backlot at MGM Studios in Culver City, California.

But I've written an alternative version. I'm not sure I will ever be satisfied with straight journalism. I want something more, something that captures the aura surrounding the story. Not the facts, but what the facts felt like. The straight story above is a façade, a front, like the storefronts on New York Avenue, and cannot reveal what goes on behind the scenes. There seems so much more to uncover, to unveil, to expose, to unravel. I want to go behind the façade. The picture of Henry Killknot in the story above is a façade, a front. That doesn't mean it's a false picture. But he has just come from wardrobe, and from makeup. He's acting. He has a role to play. So why not play around with the script a bit, especially one involving Henry Killknot? Please see the alternate version of the article below, which begins with a new title. Can you please read this version also and comment?

"Riot On New York Avenue"
By Salvador Persequi, Independent Reporter

Culver City, CA – We are in New York City, caught in a downpour. Gene Kelly appears, dancing and splashing in the puddles on New York Avenue, but he's not singing "Singin' in the Rain." He's singing Dylan's "A Hard Rain's A-Gonna Fall."

Members of the Bridge Platoon quickly subdue the aggressor Gene Kelly. They drag him away for interrogation. The simulated drill has gone smoothly, but before Lt. Henry Killknot has a chance to radio his success to Headquarters, some new disturbance seems to be breaking out.

"Hey, check it out," says Corporal Puck Malone, still fully dressed in riot control protective gear.

"Penina Seablouse," Henry Killknot says. "I don't like the looks of this."

Henry Killknot's platoon gathers under a second story window above a dress shop on New York Avenue.

Penina throws the window open, Chicago Peace roses falling from her bosom as she leans over the sill, almost falling from the window. She seems tipsy, as if she has been drinking. She is wearing a lose, white chiffon dress with tight blue straps.

"What are your names, boys?" Penina calls down.

"We're the Surf Squad, Mama," Puck Malone says.

"Penina, can I have your autograph?" Specialist Wormth asks.

"Oh, boys, I don't give autographs," Penina says.

"Chromosomal yellow," Specialist Cumbers calls up.

"Upper lip beads," Private Tino Cortez yells, smelling one of the Peace roses.

"Silence, men," Henry Killknot orders, but his men are behaving unruly.

"She gets it, man," Sergeant Humulus says. "Sure, she gets it. It's another front, man, another prop."

"What is?" Killknot asks, but his men are ignoring Henry, as some new drama begins to develop.

Penina is smiling. "Wait there, boys," Penina calls down. "I'm going to get my camera."

Killknot's men are shouting, competing for Penina's attention. They have gathered up the roses, and they are dancing now, toasting Penina with their canteens of homemade wine coolers.

"The war is over," Henry Killknot shouts up to Penina.

"Oh, it's all so good, boys, it's fine," Penina says, back in the window. "Really, you're all quite lovely."

"Penina, come down," Killknot calls.

"Really, boys, I must go back inside now," Penina says. "We've had enough excitement for one night, haven't we?"

"Bone snot!" Specialist Cumbers yells, and Killknot slaps him across the cheek.

"Oh, no!" Penina cries. "You mustn't. Not like that."

The platoon is breaking into the dress shop. The point man is in, running up the back scaffolding.

And snow starts falling on New York Avenue, in Culver City, in Los Angeles, on the backlot of the MGM studios.

"Emerald snow cologne," I tell Henry Killknot.

The platoon is now positioned in the windows above the shop fronts on New York Avenue. We hear a Dodger game broadcast from a radio somewhere up the street.

"We've failed our mission, boys," Lt. Killknot says. "God help us."

"It ain't over yet," Corporal Bubo Eyren says.

"Put a wrap on it, Bubo," Sergeant Howler orders.

"The war is over, Bubo," clerk typist Picul says, typing away at his portable typewriter set up on his lap.

Sergeant Howler leans against a lamppost and crossing his legs takes a cocktail umbrella from behind his ear and begins to pick and clean his teeth with the toothpick handle.

"I still say this war ain't over yet," Bubo insists.

"Hold your claptrap," Picul scowls at Bubo.

"Why? If the war is over, why can't we tell it like it is, let it all hang out?"

"Because I can't stop typing until you shut the hell up."

"The fin cuts true across the jelly belly," Killknot says. "The war is ended. We now must look into the whites of our own eyes and be forgotten."

The platoon grows quiet, rifles pointing out of windows, down into the street. The soft snow is falling. We see someone coming from around the corner up the street, where the aggressors earlier disappeared. Someone is on roller skates, coming our way, a woman with wavy blond hair. It is Penina Seablouse, local surfer girl from Refugio, undressed, roller-skating down the middle of New York Avenue, twirling around the overturned barricades. Henry's Bridge Platoon watches quietly as she glides past them without a glance.

Henry Killknot then pulls a letter out of his knapsack, and giving his men the "Rest" command, though they were already past rest, Cumbers and Wormth sharing a hand rolled smoke, the men drinking freely from their canteens of homemade wine cooler, Killknot reads the following letter aloud to his platoon:

"Dear Penina," Lt. Killknot reads, "From the carrots of your orange tanned toes, lined and split from sunbathing in tightly strapped rubber sandals, toenails painted purple, pink, rose orange red, angry ankles chapped from a tortured night of waitressing in roller skates in the round drive up dive joint at the end of Imperial, to the bleach blond breezy wave locked strands of your barely exposed blond root colored hair – oh, but thou art not merely a vegetable girl. The poet fails who would describe your flesh full body's achingly sweet softness, the swank padded bone, the pinkly paddled bottom, your skin covered with salt packed pores oozing oil like the seaweed bulbs we pop with our heels, walking barefoot on the beach, the kelp of the mermaid's bladder, and the aloe gel we squeeze from the cool blue flowering green plump ice plant covering the hot dunes of our soaking wet bottoms as we climb above the beach to hide and play in the swales of the warm windy dunes. The curves of your legs that dance even when still, the sculpture of your waist, free from the corset magazine museum togs, swell upward to the inevitable struggle with your raspberry ruby red drupelets whose softness disappears as my tongue like a moth burns too near the rising heat of your rising and falling breasts, two soaking full tea bags floating in peppermint and lavender. I think of you tonight, my useless mermaid swimming just beyond your wall of protective surf, all the surfers paddling to reach you, but none will make it past the breaking wall of surf, save one. The mermaid swims to shore. I meet her at the water's edge. From your blue eyes, birds crack free, emerge, their dark wings unraveling, and small sea mammals crawl out of your eyes and scurry off in search of a meal.

Love, Sal, without you tonight."

Henry looks up and wipes the back of his hand across his dirty, salt and sweat stained cheeks. The letter to Penina Seablouse he's just read falls from his hand and blows with the light snow down the street, rides an updraft over an overturned barricade, and falls and lands in a gutter. Every member of Killknot's platoon is sound asleep at his post. Somewhere in the distance a harmonica plays "Taps."

Signed: Salvador Persequi, reporting from the backlot at MGM Studios in Culver City, California.

I dreamt about you last night, Penina. You and I were sitting alone together poolside at Esther Williams's swimming pool, further west out the studio backlot. The pool was empty of water, and weeds were growing from cracks in the tiles at the bottom. We were sitting on the edge of the neglected pool. There was a bent up, rusted chaise lounge missing its cushion, hanging off the diving board. You were wearing a white cotton dress that drifted about you like curtains in the breeze of an open window. The dry smells of licorice and eucalyptus filled the air. The night was quiet, the city sleeping outside the walls of the backlot. You walked down the steps into the dry pool and danced in circles while I sat in the moonlight watching you.

Then I awoke and took out my notebook and wrote you this letter.

Love, Salty

~ ~ ~

Henry and The Punctuations

We were in an adjustment period, Penina told me. This was true. I and some other short-timers had even had a class on transitioning back into civilian life before we were discharged. "Re-entry," the class was called. I pictured myself falling from the sky into the waves off El Porto. I did not picture myself re-entering daily, casual conversations that begin obscurely and end ambiguously, but no one seeming to care. I thought about paddling across the ocean and catching a wave at El Porto, riding it to shore, and there would be Penina waiting on the beach for me with open arms. Of course she would be lovely and pure, standing in the shade of a lime green palm under a blond sun, barefoot, wearing the same white cotton dress she wore the day she saw me off to the war, the sky blue and clear, the beach empty and clean, the waves perfect green tubes, Penina's eyes like blue periwinkles. Sergeant First Class Williams warned us off fantasies, though. "Best prepare for some foggy days when you get home," he said. Sergeant Williams had looked at me and said, "Persequi, I'm worried about you, son. You're a dreamer thinks he's a thinker. Stay clear," he told me. "Stand down and stay clear."

"Jody the toady was home when you left!" Sergeant

Williams yelled, invoking the popular march cadence song, and he wouldn't let go of it. We were marching informally to our re-entry class in the half-assed, disrespectful way short timers got away with things, but Williams was having a barrel of fun with the song we hadn't sung since basic training:

"Jody was home when you left!" Sergeant Williams called out.

"So what?" came a half-hearted response.

"I can't hear you," Williams droned, elongating the "hear" and the "you."

"Susie was home when you left!" Williams snapped, even louder this time.

"Balls right!" someone screamed out.

"Sound off!" Williams yelled.

"One two three four, what the hell, we'll stay in the war."

But Penina had agreed to go out with me, so I was making re-entry progress, and around sunset a few weeks after Malone's epically petty but fateful soldier's home party, I walked down to meet Penina at her place. We'd been talking, and she was reading the new letters, but I was not sure what mood to expect, or what tone I might adopt. I climbed the steps up to her deck and knocked on the door, though it was open. The deck had been cleaned, the

122

couch with torn arms had been replaced with a couple of new, colorful beach chairs, orange and blue, and Malone's surfboard was missing from its perch, but the log roller, Penina's harpoon, still loomed on the wall above the deck.

"That you, Sal?" I heard Penina yell. "Come on in," she said, as if there had never been a fight, a party, a war.

I went in and could see her through the open bathroom door, in bra and panties, fussing with her hair and putting on some makeup. She liked to trim out her eyes. "I can't decide what to wear tonight," she said, closing the bathroom door but leaving it slightly ajar, so I could hear but not see her.

"Wear something more than you did for your New York Avenue debut," I said.

"Don't start talking crazy to me already" she said.

"Never mind," I said. "Throw on some jeans and a tee shirt."

"You know, some people do have wardrobes with more than jeans and tee-shirts."

"But you're not going to wear swim trunks to play guitar in," I said.

"What?" she said. "Please talk sense tonight, Sal."

"Just because someone is crazy doesn't mean that everything they say is crazy. Don't make me paranoid and I won't talk crazy. Did you ever read Yeats's Crazy Jane poems?"

"Crazy who?"

Penina had taught herself to play the guitar while I was away, and she had formed a folk group, herself on guitar, Peggy on banjo, and Angel adding vocals and tambourine or harmonica. I had never seen them perform, and their act did not last long, and now Penina wanted to "go solo," as she put it. Her solo debut was to be at a coffee house down in Hermosa called The Sweet End. Malone had mapped his bar crawl through the beach cities, and we were all to end up at The Sweet End to hear Penina sing her songs.

The living space we called Penina's pad was a single room efficiency apartment, a studio. That's what Malone would have called it, a studio, were he to put it up for rent. But it was a makeshift room over a garage in Refugio, noncompliant with building codes, and word of mouth was sufficient to keep such a unit occupied. Against the wall opposite the door was Penina's bed, a double, facing the beach. Next to the bed, a fully loaded bookcase stood against an inside wall that separated the bathroom from the rest of the studio apartment. There was a small writing desk to the left of the front door, beneath a window looking out onto the deck. On the desk sat a manual typewriter, some neatly stacked folders and papers, and a few books. Pushed in under the desk was a worn oak library chair. Just beyond the desk, an opening at the end of a counter led to a small utility kitchen where there was a sink and a two-burner gas stove and a small electric icebox. On the other side of the door stood a highboy dresser missing its bottom.

"Come on in," Penina said. "There's beer in the icebox. Sit down."

I had my choice of two bar stools, the library chair, a small love seat to the north of the door, or the bed. I sat down on the love seat. The apartment was clean, the bed tightly made, an acoustic guitar face up on the bed across a light blue blanket. There was a record player on a little table under the bar, and next to it a wooden crate full of albums. High on the wall above the window over the desk hung a crucifix. There was a framed photo on the wall. It was of me in my Class A's taken when I graduated from boot camp. Next to the framed photo, pinned to the wall, hung a black and white photo of me on an El Porto wave. A couple of my ink drawings were pinned to the wall above the bar. And a large "Puck's Boards" poster hung on the wall above the head of the bed. The poster showed Malone's logo above a surfboard holding a dozen stylized, stick drawn surfers in different stances, one hanging ten, another hanging five through the legs of the one hanging ten, one on the back of the board in a kick out stance, another jumping off, over the curl. And the board with all the surfers was falling down the face of a giant wave, a hill of white water following. Maybe the poster was a comment on the crowded water conditions, or an illustration of the group mentality local surfers adopt, or maybe it was just Malone's way of showing that everyone was welcome aboard his Ship of Fools. Or maybe the surfers were Penina's suitors, all falling down the face of the wave toward her bed. Below the drawing, the poster read, in block print: "Get Your Own Surfboard Custom Made at Puck Malone's Surf Shop in Refugio."

Penina came out of the bathroom dressed in a stunning, tightly fitting, Mexican wedding shirt embroidered with brilliant red-orange fantails. The shirt stopped short above a pair of hip hugging, triple bell-bottom pants, each bell a different shade of blue-green. A thin strip of tan belly showed above the pants and below the shirt, Penina's bellybutton punctuating the ensemble like an interrogation point above a faint line of slightly rusty, downy hair that led down into her pants.

My eyes had fixed on the question mark.

"Have you got a scarf or a wide belt or something you can cover up your middle with?" I asked.

"Very funny," she said. "Well?"

"Well, what?"

"You know for someone wanting to get back into good graces you sure are acting dumb," Penina said. "How do I look?"

"None too coy. I can't figure you out. Don't play pull toy."

"I'm nobody's toy."

"Coy, not toy."

"I'm not playing coy," Penina said. "I just want to look nice. And what makes you think I want to be figured out. And by the way, Henry told me you are writing me into some book. Well, you can take me out of that book you are writing," she said. "Get a real job. Make a contribution to society. Wake up in the morning, shave, put on a tie, and go lose yourself in an office somewhere. You like paperwork," Penina said.

"Are you serious?" I said. "It's not going to be much of a book if I have to take you out of it."

"I'm perfectly serious," Penina said. "Do you really imagine we can live in this one room studio apartment for the rest of our lives?"

"I must be imperfect," I said. "I don't see why not. It's just a matter of perspective."

"Are you serious?" she said. "It's a matter of small, and of tripping over one another. And of having dreams. You can write, but you have to work, too."

"I like it when we trip over one another," I said. "As for dreams, I could be locked in the tube of a wave and count myself, like Hamlet in his nutshell, a king of infinite space, were it not that I have bad dreams," I said.

"I told you not to talk like that. You are not Hamlet. I'm telling you, Sal, if you start in on that crazy stuff again you can wait outside with the rest of your hobo surf buddies. You've been home three weeks now and haven't accomplished a thing. Have you seen my songbook?" Penina was now turning books and binders over on the desk.

"What songbook?"

"Here it is. I forgot I put it in the guitar case so I wouldn't forget it."

"I think you must be nervous."

"I can't decide what song to open with. Is there a description of me in your book?"

"You want me to describe you?"

"I just asked is there one, a description. How do you describe me?"

"You mean, how do I describe who you are, what you do?"

"You know what I mean. What will I look like to your readers?"

"Ah, I see. You mean, do I tell all about your breasts of fat ripe peaches?"

"No. That is not what I mean."

"You mean, do I describe your thin, dishwater green hair and how you run your hand and fingers through it when you're upset?"

"I don't do that. And my hair is not thin. And can I help it if they put too much chorine in the plunge water?"

"You mean, do I explain how you are the most stubborn surfer girl in the South Bay?"

"I am not a surfer girl. And I am not stubborn. I'm realistic. But you still have not really described me."

"You mean, do I share the pomegranate fruit, full of lush, purple seeds, that grows between your legs and swells juicy but smells like an herb and moves like a sea anemone at the touch of a tongue?"

"You write something like that and I'll never speak to you again. I'll knock you off the rocks at the end of the jetty. You're back home now. I don't want any more letters."

"You mean, she's five feet and four inches tall, medium build, broad shoulders of a swimmer, somewhat flat behind, but when she sticks it out playfully, leaning forward, toes splayed, lifting her feet off her heels, one hand behind her head, her peaches fuzzy forward, the other hand on her lilting rump, one notices ample muscles in her calves and thighs and around her waist. She appears to eat well, but is not fat, but her face is cherubic, slightly pronounced cheekbones reddened from the sun with a few brown freckles under powder blue eyes beneath strong eyebrows. She takes cute photographs because before the shutter clicks she has a habit of grabbing one side of her bottom lip between her teeth in an endearing self-conscious smile, as if the camera is about to take something from her that she both wants to give and wants to keep. Her face is full, and she wears a not unhappy smile when she's not thinking of her past, but it's a knowing smile, knowledge of something hidden, something that lives deep within a seashell, like a sound. She protects the secret from the wind and surf as if it were a child, a child listening."

"Enough," Penina said flatly.

"And her skin is pearl, like the pearl of a shell rose tan from the sun, smooth but slightly salty and covered with fine down sun bleached hairs."

"Enough, I said."

"Shall I tell about the time I washed with my tongue the sweet soft skin on the inside of your thighs, and you said, 'You're driving me crazy'?"

"I never said that. You're the crazy one, and I'm serious

about that."

"What about surfing?" I said.

"What about it?"

"I've been surfing for three weeks, and shaping boards up at Puck's. What do you mean I haven't accomplished anything? Maybe a guy who does nothing but surf every day is doing society a big favor. And another thing I've accomplished. I visited Tom Chippy's parents. And now I've been going back over there and helping get Ray out of the house. We've been down to the beach, taking a few walks, enjoying one another's company."

"Well, that's nice. I'm glad to hear you are helping Ray."

"Listen to this. I've been reading this musician, John Cage, 'How to Improve the World: You'll Only Make Matters Worse.' I found it up at Malone's place, your name on the inside cover, by the way. Anyway, think about it. Every morning I surf, I'm at least not out in the world screwing something up. That's doing society a favor," I said.

"Speaking on behalf of society," Penina said, "don't do us any favors."

"But you just said I should be making a contribution to society," I said.

"You know what? You're right. Go surfing. Get out of the house. You'll be doing society and me a favor. What songs should

I sing tonight?"

"How about 'Society's Child'?" I said.

"Peggy says I should sing my own songs."

"Speaking of society," I said, "I've been doing some thinking."

"I wish you wouldn't do that," Penina said.

"Do what?"

"Think. That's your problem. You think too much. I thought you were going surfing."

"I'm not going surfing. I'm going with you. What are you talking about?"

"I have to get ready for tonight. I want to run through my songs once more before we go."

"You're nervous, aren't you? That's your problem. You're irritable because you're nervous about singing tonight," I said.

"You're so perceptive. Are you going to write a music review for me, for the newspaper?"

"Of course. I brought my notebook. Yes, but listen. It's been very interesting, you know, coming home and looking at how much things have changed."

"I thought you said nothing has changed."

"I said you have changed."

"I thought you said people don't change."

"I changed my mind about that."

"You're driving me crazy with this silly palaver. Go away."

"Palaver, sounds like the name of a bird," I said.

Penina stared down at me, sitting on the couch. She was beautiful.

"I don't know what to say," I said.

"Really? Master letter writer at a loss for words, huh? How about, you look nice, Penina."

"You look nice, Penina."

"Thank you, Salvador. Are you going to listen to a few songs, then?"

"No, no, wait. Please, I want to talk to you. Explain to me what's going on, please."

"What's going on is, we're going up to meet Puck and company, and we're all heading out for an evening of music and frivolity. That's all."

"That's it?"

"Why, what were you thinking?"

"What's frivolity mean?" I said.

"I don't know," she said. "I guess it could mean anything from simple fun to acting like fools."

"You feel like acting the fool?" I said.

"No," she said. "I've had enough foolishness. How about you?"

"No," I said. "Some would say I've been playing the fool, and it's time to sober up."

"Stand up," Penina said. "I'm going to give you something to sober you up."

I stood up, and she came toward me and put her arms around me and kissed me. Her hair smelled like fresh, baseball card bubblegum. Her lips were wet and warm, and she opened her mouth and slid her tongue into mine and withdrew it slowly and rubbed it across my lips. She stopped and pulled away and looked at me, smiling, periwinkle eyes spinning, but I started to cry. It was a foolish, childish, but maybe soldierly thing to do. In any case, I could not help myself. I fell back onto the couch, and I could not stop crying. I could not breathe. I was sobbing.

"If this is an act," Penina said, "I'll open that scar back up with my harpoon."

She sat down next to me and put her arms around me. We sat in silence for a few minutes. I calmed down. I suddenly felt exhausted.

"What's the matter?" she said.

"I don't know," I said.

"Listen," she said, "we've been through this. I love you, but I don't know what I want. I guess I must want something more than love, but I'm not sure what that is."

I was quiet, and after awhile I said, "That wasn't very soldierly of me. Sorry."

"You think we don't know that soldiers cry? Anyway, you're not a soldier anymore," she said. "Besides, you think I don't know all you bad ass surfers are just jellyfish floating helplessly under those fake shells?"

"I just want to surf and make love with you," I said. "It's all I thought about through the whole war. It's what got me through."

"Well, you still have surfing," she said, smiling.

"Funny," I said.

"Love isn't something you make," Penina said. "I tried making love with Puck Malone, and it was like manufacturing gadgets, like I was moving down an assembly line. Giggle here, giggle there, turn this, twist that, and wham, bam, thank you mam, every ride the same. Is that what surfing is like?"

"That's nonsense and anyway doesn't make me feel better," I said.

"Once, I swear, it was like Puck was paddling, and he jumps up, like he's up on the board, on a wave now. I think he must have been fantasizing about a wave."

"Enough. Wait, once? And did you say, every ride? How many Penina waves did Puck catch while I was away?"

"Never mind. He wiped out. But that little outburst of yours just now isn't about Puck and me" she said.

"I don't know," I said. "Maybe not."

"Listen," Penina said, "we need to come to an understanding. This ideal lover idea you have of me isn't the same idea I have of myself."

"What idea?"

"I'm not a saint. I'm not all blue and white inside," Penina said. "There's a lot of deep purple and neon oranges and fire engine reds. And sometimes I wake up in a field of yellow green pee sea. And I smell, sometimes, and sweat. I have body odor. I burp. I don't shave my legs anymore, or my armpits. And my hair is not really blond. My father was a drunk, and my mother went crazy."

"I don't know what you're talking about. Are you turning into a Van Gogh or Picasso painting?"

"Very funny. You think you're the only one who can wax poetic? Anyway, the point is, love is one thing, living together, something else. Sometimes I think it might be better to live with someone we don't love, or don't love so much. Anyway, wanting to be with someone because you are afraid to sleep alone is not love," Penina said. "And why does love have to be so serious?"

"Yes," I said. "And why does love have to be so tough?"

"I don't want to wind up like my mom," Penina said.

"What does your mom have to do with anything?"

"The sex we had in high school was kid's stuff. Now it's all serious. Malone's having trouble transitioning from introductory to advanced sex, but he sure thinks he's some sort of expert or something."

"You lost me again. What the hell. Are you getting a degree in sex education, or what?"

"I'm afraid if we have sex it will ruin everything."

"And you think I'm the romantic? I think maybe you're the one putting on an act, playing games," I said.

"You okay now? You want something to drink? You want another beer?" Penina said.

"No, thanks."

"Should I light up a joint?"

"No."

"What do you want to do?"

"I don't know. It's doesn't matter. It's almost time to go, now."

"You going to be ok?

"Yeah, I'm fine."

We heard someone on the stairs, and they were on the deck.

"Penina?" a woman's voice called out.

"Oh, God," Penina said. "It's Donna.

"Who?"

"A neighbor, Donna Jabanoso."

"Hi, Donna," Penina called out. "Come on in."

A small, middle-aged woman came through the door, and Castus ran out.

"Oh, I'm sorry. I let the cat out, and I didn't know you had company," she said.

"It's okay. Castus can go out. This is Sal. You haven't met him yet. Sal, this is Donna Jabanoso. She lives on the other side of Puck's place."

"Hello, Salvador," Donna Jabanoso said. "I've heard so much about you. Welcome back. I'm glad you are home, safe and sound. That silly war, oh, my gosh," Donna Jabanoso said. "Am I interrupting anything?" she asked.

"We're supposed to go out in a little while. I'm playing at The Sweet End tonight, down in Hermosa."

"Oh, good for you. Well, I was just out for a little walk.

I'm so upset."

"What's wrong?" Penina asked.

"Have you heard about John's separation?"

"No."

"It's terrible, and just when he's found out his wife is pregnant by his ex-boss."

"You've got to be kidding."

"No. I'm dead serious. And, it looks like their older son, Manny, from Mary's prior marriage, is dropping out of college and wants to be a priest. Can you imagine such a thing? You just wait and see," Donna Jabanoso said. "I told him, but priests go to college, too. Think about all those rules they have to learn. It's got to be almost as bad as being a lawyer."

I waited for Penina to respond, but she was looking down, running her hand through her hair. I did not know these people Donna Jabanoso was talking about.

"But I just stopped by to say hello. I don't want to hold you kids up," Donna Jabanoso said, as she sat down on one of the bar stools. "I don't suppose you have a bottle of wine open, do you? I could really use a little drink. You know how Michael doesn't like me drinking too early. Of course that doesn't apply to him. But he's taken to hiding my stash – I call it my stash, you know – but it's not marijuana. Don't get the wrong idea," Donna

Jabanoso said, laughing. "I'm way too old for that refer madness stuff. Besides, Michael would divorce me in a heartbeat if he ever found out I had taken even a little puff off of a – what do you call it? A joint. Speaking of cigarettes, do you mind if I smoke?"

"Here, let me get you an ashtray and a little glass of wine," Penina said. "But then we should probably get going, not to be rude or anything."

Donna Jabanoso looked around forty years old, maybe a little older. Her hair was short and tightly curled, and she was wearing floral pedal pushers and sandals and a big floppy blouse. The skin on her face was tightly tanned. It looked like leather about to break into wrinkles.

"Oh, thank you, Penina," she said, as Penina poured a glass of wine and set out an ashtray.

"Oh, they just have so many problems, the parents and the children. I just don't know where it will all end. I swear I don't," Donna Jabanoso said.

"Of course, they are not really your problems," Penina said.

"Well, I'm so glad you are back safe and sound, Salvador," Donna Jabanoso said. "Is it all right if I call you Salvador? What do you like to be called?"

"Not too many people call me Salvador," I said. "I usually

140

just go by Sal."

"Well, you can call me Donna, or Donnie, or Don. I answer to just about anything. I swear," Donna said, with a laugh that broke into a cough. "I don't know how the world keeps on turning, all of us having to walk in these dark shadows, the shadows of the war and all. Penina, where's your letterbox of Salvador's letters? I don't see it here on the bar where you always used to keep it. Where is it?"

Penina stared at me as if the world had stopped turning, her eyes retreating in dark shadows, speaking of shadows.

"It got lost," Penina said.

"Lost!" Donna Jabanoso hissed. "What do you mean it got lost?"

"It's a long story," Penina said.

"Penina used to read those letters every night," Donna Jabanoso said. "She never showed me one, though. I said to her, 'Penina, does that much really happen on a daily basis that he has that much to say about the war and all?' And she said, 'well, he doesn't really write about the war all that much.' And I said, 'well, what does he write about, then?' And Penina, I swear, her eyes rolled into the back of her head, but she never did answer that question."

"Well, it's a long story, and kind of personal," Penina said.

"Is it a long story when you tell what happened to the letters, too, Salvador?" Donna Jabanoso said.

"Longer, much longer, too long," Penina said. "Listen, why don't you come down to The Sweet End and listen tonight?" Penina asked Donna Jabanoso.

"Oh, my gosh, I don't know. Michael doesn't like going out, you know. I'll ask him, though. He likes you, Penina, and he's been keen to meet Salvador here, having heard so much about him. We kept up with the war on television, Sal, you bet we did."

She seemed to be waiting for me to say something. "Well, thank you," I said.

"And that boy friend of Penina's, what's his name?"

"Puck?"

"No, no, not Puck, God love him, the big rascal. That other one, tall, awkward, gawky kid, the one with the red sports car, lives right across the way, though I don't see him that often."

"Henry," Penina said.

"Yes, yes, that's it, Henry. Odd boy, but anyway, he used to keep me up to date on the latest developments, you know, stuff the news could not say, he said, you know, state secrets, and such. Why, he is an officer in the National Guard," Donna Jabanoso said. "And so smart, like a shark, mind like a shark, quiet and quick, a loner. That's who buys those fancy sport cars, that's what

Michael said."

Donna Jabanoso was now practically hidden in smoke, as if a fog had rolled in, but she soon finished her cigarette and glass of wine and went noisily out and back down the stairs, and Penina and I went up to meet Malone and the others for the trip down to The Sweet End.

"I guess I should have said I was sorry to hear about so many problems in Mrs. Jabanoso's family," I said, wanting to respond in some way to what appeared to be the woman's woeful life experience.

"What family?" Penina said.

"Well, all the problems with the relatives she was just describing," I said.

"She's wasn't talking about her real family," Penina explained, laughing, one hand on her stomach, the other over her mouth. "She was talking about her soap operas, on television, though I can understand how you could draw that conclusion. I'm sometimes not sure she understands the soaps are not real," Penina said.

"No kidding," I said. "Soap operas. I wonder who writes that stuff."

"We don't have to go on this silly Malone music cruise,

you know," Penina said. "We can just go down to The Sweet End on our own and hang out there until it's time for me to sing."

"I'm looking forward to hearing your songs," I said.

"It's all acoustic, but I'll have two microphones, one for the vocals and one for the guitar. Do you think you'll be able to hear? I mean, I don't want you to hurt your ears anymore."

"I should be fine. The waves are flat today."

"I'm nervous."

"What songs did you decide to sing?"

"You want to hear one now?"

I had not been to The Sweet End, but I got the lowdown from Penina. It was a small club off of Pier Avenue, in Hermosa. The Sweet End was a candle lit, incense burning, and sawdust on softwood floor, folk revival coffee house. A small, floor level stage area provided aspiring musicians an open-mike chance to air their songs in front of a friendly audience of twenty to forty patrons. A couple of waitresses worked the tables serving coffee and tea or sodas with pastries and pies or fruits and cheeses. The alley out back offered shadowed shelter for those in need of a joint or had a brown bag bottle to share. Hermosa's cops ignored the alley as long as they didn't get any nuisance or noise abatement complaints. The Sweet End was the least of their problems.

Besides, one of the cops with two of the county lifeguards had formed a bodacious barn-burning trio of guitar, banjo, and acoustic bass, and they regularly shook the place. But they were not on the bill the night I followed Penina down with her guitar and songbook in hand for her solo folk debut. The Sweet End was to be the last stop on Malone's bar crawl.

Penina and I jumped ahead of Malone's crew to get to The Sweet End early so she could get a good spot on the open microphone sign up sheet. We got there around eight, and she seemed happy to get a ten o'clock slot, which gave Malone and friends time to catch up with us without missing her songs. Occasionally, The Sweet End opened its microphone to poets and others of similar, soapbox needs. What this meant in practice is that if someone who wanted to perform brought a few paying customers along, the club was happy to hand the mike over. When Penina and I arrived, about twenty or so folkies were listening to a giant man with a huge gut and boiled over face reciting guttural, gutter full poems about lewd or lonely women lurking in boxcar bars, the poet hero drawn to their drunken siren songs. His voice sounded smoke and drink damaged as he spewed cuss word adjectives, coupling them to innocent nouns in phrases that might have made Drill Sergeant Haett blush.

Penina knew who the poet was, but I did not. He was

known locally as Big Poet, and she said he'd be famous some day, this on the strength of the say-so of a Mr. Gabbia, one of the English teachers out at El Camino, a favorite of Penina's, who happened to be in the audience, and Penina excitedly introduced me to him, and he invited us to join him at his table. He introduced us to a Mr. Buckett, who was also sitting at the table. Over all of this, the extra-thick honeyed voice of the gut poet droned, to the evident delight of Misters Gabbia and Buckett.

"I've heard a lot about you," Mr. Gabbia said. "Penina tells me you've just returned from the war."

"What war?" Mr. Buckett said, smiling slyly, avoiding eye contact with me.

"Good question," I said. "It could have been any of them, including the next one."

"Sadly so," Mr. Buckett said.

"Penina said you've been doing some writing," Mr. Gabbia said.

Big Poet rattled off some invectives. He was like a jackhammer, shaking the place up, his voice like metal hammering concrete. We paused to watch and listen as he alliterated off a string of F-words. The audience seemed not very attentive.

"I imagine you heard a fair amount of cussing in the war zone," Mr. Buckett said.

"Maybe," I said, "but not usually gratuitous. One learns not to waste bullets."

"Really?" Mr. Gabbia said, incredulous, "no cussing in a bloody, shit stained war?"

"Have you ever been in a war?" I asked.

"No, can't say as I have."

"The experience of war can not be told in words," I said, "but when F-words fill the cheeks with froth, a fascist has infiltrated the mind."

"Who the fuck talks like that?" Buckett scrunched his eyebrows over scowling lips.

"My friend, Henry," I said. "It's a game we play."

"Clever," Gabbia said. "But getting back to the common foot soldier, surely words like fuck and shit are as common as cigarettes and coffee. Part of his mess kit, I shouldn't wonder."

"That's right," I said. "And, like the mess, rationed."

"But surely the unfixed tongue is one of the few freedoms the foot soldier feels, and in the fire of the fight, is a weapon he can unleash to gratify his fear."

"To be frank, no," I said. "But, the foot soldier does make efficient and effective use of his F-word vocabulary."

"Do tell," Gabbia said.

"Shouldn't we be listening to the poet?" I asked.

"Listen. Don't listen. Tune in. Tune out," Gabbia said. "Big Poet could care less. I'm surprised he's not fully turned his back on his audience this evening."

"I knew a guy, Snippy," I said, leaning forward, moving quickly into a story. "We called him Snippy because he used to get out ahead of us to ferret out snipers, and because he was our F-word expert. One day, we're making our way blindly forward, Snippy up ahead, and we hear a muffled explosion and a cry like some wounded bird, and we hear a hissing sound. We fan out, and I'm the first to reach Snippy, hearing and smelling my way toward him, and I find that his legs have been blown away. One leg is off to the side, the other is hanging from a tree. He's like the scarecrow in the Wizard of Oz after the flying monkeys have had their way with him. Snippy is crying softly, whimpering, but pounding the ground with his arms and fists, his torso wiggling. He looks down to see his penis hanging free, flopping about at the bottom of his wiggling, flopping torso. 'Oh, Jesus' he moans slowly. 'Oh, no, no, no,' he starts shouting, getting louder and louder, a crescendo of nos. Then he yells, 'Oh, no, Jesus, no,' and he lets out wheeze after wheeze, not really saying anything, but breathing hard, and he yells, not wanting it to be happening, but it is happening, 'Oh, Jesus, help me.' Then he sees me. 'Salty,' he yells. 'Salty, where's Suzie? Get my photo of Suzie. It's in my wallet in the side pocket of my pants, hanging from the tree.' Then he starts yelling for his girlfriend, like he's angry with her. Why doesn't she help him? Why won't she help him? And he yells at me. 'Salty, why don't you help me?' he yells. 'Oh, Suzie, Oh, Salty,' he cries. He's arching his back up with his arms, trying to get up, his eyes rolling around. I sit down next to him, try to calm him, feel his pulse, and check his legs, his stumps. He doesn't appear to be bleeding much. The blast has cauterized his wounds. But he is bleeding, and has lost blood. 'Medic,' I shout. 'No,' Snippy says. 'This is my final fiddle,' Sal. I'm a fuzzer, about to freak out. It's been a frolic. Sorry to fail you. I'm about to freeze.' Then he falls back, and his one leg falls from the tree and hits the ground with a thud, and suddenly, he's fuck off fuck all fuck dead. I take one of his dog tags and put it in my pocket, and take the wallet out of his pants and pull out Suzie's photo. She's a dish. I empty his wallet into my pockets, not much there, a letter, his ID. One by one the rest of the squad reaches us. A silence falls, everyone out of breath, sitting now under the tree, keeping Snippy company. Bubo, our rear guard, finally catches up with us, takes a look around, and says, long and slow and reckoning, 'Far out.'"

"And the clichéd point of this sad soldier's tale?" Bucket asked, feigning a look of exaggerated boredom.

"Snippy never said a cuss word. I never heard Snippy utter

one single cuss word. Don't say Snippy had a foul mouth because he was a foot soldier. The F-word for that, by the way, is infantry. As for all the F-words Snippy passed as he was dying, they were all codes."

"Codes for what?" Gambia yelled at me.

"If I pass you the codes, I fail my squad, and I fear I would be forced to Faustus you."

"What the fuck?" Bucket yelled.

Penina was pulling on my arm, and I looked around to see the coffee shop was quiet, and everyone was looking over at our table. The big guy at the microphone was quiet.

"Come on, Sal," Penina said. "Let's go outside and cool off."

"What?" I said.

I looked at Big Poet at the microphone, and saw him take a flask from his hip pocket and take off the cap and throw back his head, taking a long swig, and he replaced the cap and put the flask back in his pocket. I stood up with Penina. Gabbia and Buckett were looking up at me.

"What's the matter?" I asked Penina. "What happened?"

"You just got a little loud, that's all," Penina said. "Let's go outside and get some fresh air."

"I got a little loud?"

"Come on. Let's go outside."

We went outside and sat at one of the small tables set up on the sidewalk.

"You okay?"

"Yes, yes. Why? What happened in there?"

"You told a story, and, well, you got really loud at the end. You were yelling," Penina said.

"Jesus."

"Yeah. You okay, now?"

"Yes. Should I go back in and apologize or something?"

"Not or something. I think it's okay. I think everyone understands," Penina said. "Why don't we just sit out here for a little while and watch the cars and people go by."

One of the waitresses came outside and asked us did we want something to drink, and Penina asked her to bring me a glass of water.

"Maybe we should go home," Penina said. "I could take you back home."

"No," I said. "I want you to sing your songs. What do you mean, I was yelling? I was just telling them a story."

Penina pulled her chair over next to mine. She took a napkin off the table and wiped my eyes and cheeks.

"Did you know you are crying?" she asked.

"I am?"

"Well, these look like tears to me," Penina said, rubbing my cheeks with the napkin.

"I'm okay," I said. "I'll be okay."

"What happened, Sal? What were you thinking?"

"I'm not sure. I'm not sure I like these Gabbia and Buckett types."

"Oh, they're okay. I think you're just being a little sensitive. It's probably going to take a little more time to adjust to guys like them."

"I never really knew any guys like them, so sarcastic, so cynical."

"No, probably not. Except maybe one of your best friends, Henry."

"It's an interesting word, adjust," I said. "Get things right, the right fit. Make things right. Correct wrongs. Carpenter's plane. Shave. Razor. Shim. Shim it in. Shim it up. Shim it out. Shimmy."

"Sal, stop. You have to make an effort here," Penina said. "Please, please don't talk crazy, for me, okay?"

"I promise," I said. "But what do you promise?"

"I promise I will help you when you really need help."

"I was just saying how adjust is an interesting word. Just. Justice. Just ice cubes. An ice cube would make a nice adjustment to this water."

"Sal."

"Okay, okay. Just kidding. Let's go back inside."

"You sure?"

"Yes, I'm good. Besides, anyway, I was just kidding. I made the whole story up. I never knew a guy named Snippy. And I for sure never saw anyone with their legs blown off like that."

"Are you kidding me? I'm not sure if that makes this better or worse." Penina sat back in her chair and looked hard at me, as if asked to make a diagnosis of some sort.

"I'm not sure, either," I said. "It just came out, like I was astral travelling, an out of body experience."

"So why would you make something like that up?"

"I don't know. Actually, I did know a guy named Snippy. William. Willy Snippy. Nice guy. And he did die. A good man. And he did have a girl friend. But I don't think her name was Suzie. Matilda, maybe. Anyway, one day, he opens a letter from Matilda, and it's a Dear John letter. Next leave, old Snippy got drunk and fell out of a cathouse window into the street below. Broke his neck, face down on the pavement he hit. Street urchins on him like he'd fallen into a nest of yellow jackets, picking his pockets clean."

"Jesus, Sal," Penina said, shaking her head and running a

153

hand through her hair. "I don't know what to believe, anymore."

I finished my water, and Penina sat with me, and we watched the crowd, all kinds of folks walking back and forth on Pier Avenue. A couple of skaters strolled clumsily along, and a kid on a skateboard, and a blond hair girl in a blue dress riding a blue bicycle rode slowly by and gave me a big smile and I nodded and smiled back at her. A couple of longhairs with backpacks stopped and asked if we had any change, and I gave them a dollar bill. Across the street, a group wearing saffron robes and banging tambourines started singing with a shuffle a chant. I could not hear the surf in the distance. I tried to pick it up. After a little while, Penina suggested we might go back inside The Sweet End.

We went back inside. Penina said we should go back to Gabbia's table, so I could see they were decent, ordinary guys.

"Okay," I said, "but if either one of those guys mentions my feet again, I'm going to break someone's nose."

"Sal, that is not even funny."

"I have two perfectly normal feet. Well, as normal as one might expect for someone who has been walking across broken glass for a couple of years and has seen more than your average professor has ever imagined."

"You know, no one gets those constant allusions you're

prone to," Penina said, stopping, putting her hand on my chest, "except Henry, maybe, and me, sometimes, and if you can't find the Jesus hiding inside others, including the professors, then what you have seen hasn't done you much good, after all, has it?"

"Fine, let us continue our visit with the rotting Guildenstern and goading Rosencrantz, who seem to share a Jesus. Goad to stern. Rot in pants."

"Jesus, Sal, really? What am I going to do with you?"

We sat back down at Gabbia and Buckett's table, but before much could be said, Big Poet, with the bulbous, boiling nose, came over and plopped himself down at our table, and taking out his flask, asked me if I could use a hit.

"How you feeling, man?" Big Poet said.

"I'm okay," I said. "I guess I owe you an apology for getting a little carried away during your reading."

"Nah, no way, man. What the hell. You were on fire. You were smoking the place up. You beat the shit out of me, man. Good job."

"Well, just the same, I'd like to apologize," I said, and held out my hand for him to shake.

"They call me Banzai Hunkaroo when I'm down here hunched up in the beach cities," he said. "Though I seldom come down this way for fear of drifting beerless out on some deserted beach bereft of Penina type angles who would sing to me a high tide lullaby and let me taste cool drinking beer from the cleavage of their big flopping tits." He leaned back roaring with laughter that turned into a coughing fit.

I looked at Penina, my mouth open, and saw that she was smiling, not embarrassed.

"That's just his way," Penina said to me, and reached out and took my hand in hers, and I suddenly felt transported, though I wasn't yet sure to where. I thought I might just make it though this evening of frivolity without drowning in small talk.

"The man built the war," Big Poet said, "built the war machine, you see, a frightful jumbo monster child munching machine, an olive drab green roller coaster, every seat filled with a Government Issue Jack and his buddy, Thomas Mix or Hucklessberry Finn. And they all ride to war on this Pike-like roller coaster, arms in the air over their heads, while all the Peninas are left behind pining and whining and sighing, loop to loop to loo to toodedly do." Big Poet took another swig from his flask.

"And the sweet lass Penina," he said, "with the fin-like ass must endure the lure of fame crawling up her thigh, the handiwork of a handy professor of the Humanities who did not go to war but stayed home, stayed in bed, in fact, slept through the whole war long, waking up just long enough to teach a few Wilfred Owen poems to the young boys awaiting their draft notices, and this he considered his duty, the penis pinched bastard."

"Who are your influences?" Buckett interrupted, asking the poet.

"Falstaff," Big Poet said. "And I don't mean the Shakespeare character. I mean the beer. Speaking of which, what do you say, Salty, my newfound good buddy, we go find ourselves a nice quiet table in the far dark shadows of a reputable beach dive, where the flies are fat, and I'll treat you, you crazy bastard with no book to call home, to some serious suds, to some white capped piss building suds. Uh? What say ye, me Billy, to a walk along the dock in search of a warm wet seat to dock our big hard telephone pole long cocks for the evening?"

I looked again at Penina. She ran a hand through her hair, looking down at the table. Gabbia and Buckett could no longer hold the fake serious poses they had struck when Penina and I had come back into The Sweet End. They smiled, then laughed, and at that point our table broke into a wave of laughter, Big Poet loud and boisterous, his eyes nearly closed as his fat, swollen cheeks expanded across his face in a horrendous grin. I also laughed, joining the game. Big Poet leaned his torso across the table and stuck his face into each of ours in turn, at each face letting out a bellow or a scream, a hoot or toot. I laughed too, and met his hoot to me with a return guffaw. But Penina still had hold of my hand, and she was not laughing.

Our table quieted down again, and Big Poet lit off on a soliloquy.

"I've not laughed so hard since my gone gal go-go gone-gone gonorrhea left me for a right prick of a best friend," Big Poet said. "What the hell was his name? Tad. No, Toe. That was it, big bad tad Toe. This I have learned, for which I've spent my heart, there isn't any night that can't be beat with a pack of cigs, a case of cool ones, and a sturdy steel typewriter setup with a brand spanking new glossy black ribbon wound round as tight as Penina's politely folked pussy lined with fresh panties the color of that dark black ribbon, panties that glow in the black light of a black moon penetrating a dark room, Salty's big as a rocket to the moon cock beating full of blood muscle fuel slow but bright like the lamp of a lighthouse, the hard yet soft head sounding blip...bleep...blop... in the slow dark fog of a wet doggy fuck."

There might have been more, but he was overcome by a coughing fit that he staunched with another swig from his flask.

I looked at Penina again. She looked at me and smiled, still holding my hand, running her other hand through her hair. Big Poet put his arm around her, laughing, his armpit drenched with sweat. He pulled Penina over to him and gave her a kiss on the top of her head. One thing seemed certain. Big Poet had got the best of Buckett and Gabbia. They sat quietly by, smiling politely at Big Poet's antics, unsure how to handle a live poet loose from their library.

"Don't worry, Salty, my friend. That's as close a taste of Penina as I've ever had or ever will. Have you ever noticed, by the by, how her hair smells sweetly and thickly of baseball card bubble gum? Penina is a poem you'll not fit in a book, Mr. Gabbia," Big Poet said. "She is a folk song, indeed, a lovely breeze floating over a deep, secret sea."

"Yes," I said, looking at Penina. "Yes. That is something I might have said. Penina is a sea rising up in waves to meet the breeze," I said, looking now at Big Poet.

"Penina Seablouse arouses the sea deep within me," Big Poet said.

"Yes," I said. "Penina stirs the seaweed drifting in the pit of my stomach," I said, "the seagrass at the bottom of my stomach."

"Yes," Big Poet said. "Penina Seablouse sings of the loosened whale sounding the depth of my innards."

"Is this the same Penina, sitting here?" I said.

"No," Big Poet said, looking at Penina. "I seem to have

made a mistake. The Penina Seablouse I knew had black hair, hair the color of coal, the black of beach tar. But this Penina, the lure of fame is crawling up her thigh. She'd better pull down her skirt and cover her thighs."

"Let's have a song, now, Penina," Mr. Buckett said. "I for one would welcome a change in the course of this conversation, so to speak."

"It's not my time," Penina said. "Another singer should be coming on now."

"I fear they have skedaddled addled out of here," Big Poet said, "bashful now in the light of your heralded voice."

"It's getting late. The others seem not to be coming," Penina said. "I wonder where Malone is," Penina said to me. "It's getting late, too late. I think I may not want to sing, after all" Penina said.

"It's never too late to start singing," Big Poet said.

Big Poet stood up and banged the table to regain the attention of the small crowd. "Lords and gentlewomen and hard ones too," Big Poet yelled at the room, "Banzai Bill Big Poet Hunkster here again introducing to you the lovely without further dew drops the doo-wopping stop the show folkster, Penina Seablouse!" And he started to clap and sway back and forth and came around to lift Penina up and escort her across the room to the stage.

Penina's guitar was strung across her shoulder, and she stepped up to the microphone. The crowd settled down, Big Poet came back to our table, and we waited in anticipation. Penina introduced herself and her song. "Hello, everyone. My name is Penina Seablouse, which you probably know by now, thanks to my friend Big Poet. My song is called 'Uniforms,' and is dedicated to my friend Salty, just returned from the war. But I guess you've figured that out too, if you've been listening to our table the last little while."

I felt a few people staring at me, and Big Poet slapped me on my back, shaking his head up and down in approval. Penina's song was a surprise.

She strummed a few chords, closed her eyes, and began to sing in a slow, soft, carefully measured voice, after each short verse playing different notes and chord sequences on her guitar, stepping back from the microphone, as if the better to let her words fill the space, before continuing with the next verse:

The boy becomes a man, Penina sang,
dresses down in green.
Off he goes to march

in his starched uniform.

His girl becomes a woman,
a waitress in a red apron.
They each have orders
to satisfy others.

Walking in parade,
he puts her on a float.
She waves and waves,
on his back a goat.

A knock at the door.
The man in his uniform
needs her no more.

I wasn't sure if Penina's song was over or not, for just
then a commotion at the door to The Sweet End distracted
everyone in the crowd and Penina stopped playing. And in through
the door came marching in line Henry Killknot, Puck Malone,
John Humulus, and Lucas Crux. Killknot carried a cardboard sign
on which was handwritten "The Punctuations, a Folksong
Quartet," and as they came in, they were singing a cockeyed

version of the old folk song "When Johnny Comes Marching Home Again."

"When Sally comes marching home again," Killknot sang.

"Surf's Up! Surf's Up!" the others sang in unison.

"We'll give him a hearty welcome then," sang Killknot.

"Banzai! Banzai!" shouted the others.

"Surfers will cheer, and hodads will shout,

The surfer girls they will all turn out,

And we'll all feel gay

When Sally comes marching home," Killknot sang.

The four of them now occupied the stage, poor Penina pushed to the rear.

"The old black ball, pull down with joy," Killknot sang.

"Hang five! Hang five!" the others returned.

"To welcome home our darling Sal," sang Killknot.

"Kick out! Kick out!" Malone, Crux, and Humulus yelled.

"The beach lads and lassies say

With seashells they will strew the way,

And we'll all feel gay

When Sally comes marching home," Killknot sang.

"Get ready for the surfing fest," Killknot continued, arms spread toward the crowd, waving his cardboard sign.

"Hurrah! Hurrah!"

"We'll see the hero paddling out."

"Hurrah! Hurrah!"

"The seaweed wreath is ready now
To place upon his hollow brow,
And we'll all feel gay
When Sally comes marching home."

"Let hugs and kisses on that day,"

"Say hey, say Sal!"

"Penina's pleasures then display,"

"Say Sal, say hey!"

"And let each one perform some part,
To fill with joy the warrior's heart,
And we'll all feel gay when
Sally comes marching home,"

"When Sally comes marching home," they all joined in.

"When Sally comes marching home."

They came off the little stage of The Sweet End, and they

lifted me up onto Killknot and Malone's shoulders, we squeezed through the door, and they carried me on their shoulders, down Pier Avenue, and walked me out onto the Hermosa Beach Pier, all the while continuing to sing improvised verses of "When Sally Comes Marching Home," Malone, Killknot, Crux, and Humulus, a rowdy crowd building in their wake. They carried me out to the end of the pier. A few fishermen with lines in the water, their five gallon buckets half full of water, paused to look and shake their heads in disbelief. We passed a couple of Jesus freaks evangelizing a few longhaired kids smoking joints on a bench. And at the end of the pier, at the end of a last hurrah, they threw me over the rail and off the pier and I fell flapping into the water.

I remember falling from the pier, the water rising to take me. When I awoke, I was on the beach, Malone over me performing mouth-to-mouth resuscitation, the spotlight of a county lifeguard truck illuminating the circle of a crowd, with me in the center of the spotlight. I rolled over and vomited a pint of seawater. I rolled back up, and Malone was walking in a circle around me, his arms in the air, the crowd cheering their hero, for Puck had saved my life by diving in after me, pulling me away from the pier pilings.

"Never a doubt! Never a doubt!" Malone shouted, and the crowd sent up another cheer as Killknot and Humulus picked me up and laid me in the back of the lifeguard truck, and we rode up to the main tower at the end of the pier.

It was after midnight when I got back to my room above Puck's surf shop, and I found Penina asleep on my bed. She didn't wake up. Her guitar case was leaning against the bed, closed. I sat down at my desk and watched her sleep. I climbed into bed next to her, but still she did not awake. I fell asleep, and in the morning, when I woke up, she was gone, and her guitar was gone, too. I got out of bed and went to the window to check out the surf, but on my desk I found a note: "You can come down and sleep with me at my place tonight. One night at a time. Don't be crazy. You scare me when you go loco. Love, Penina."

I went down to the shop and made some coffee. Malone was nowhere around. I went back up to my room to do some writing. I wrote Penina another letter.

Dear Penina:

I woke up and you were gone, but I found your note, which I've already framed in silver and gold and screwed to the wall over my desk. I was thinking later I might drive it to a bank over in El Segundo and stash it in a safe deposit box. But on the wall over my desk it will give me inspiration and motivation and encouragement and support and ideas to write and shape and have something to look forward to while working all day. But about what you call crazy stuff, I should probably say something about that. I don't want you to worry too much.

Then again, I really don't know what to say about it, other than what I've already told you. Maybe acting crazy is a survival strategy. Maybe actually going crazy is a survival strategy. How does one know the difference? It's risky. I think I'm just tired. I liked your song, though. I'd like to talk to you some about the lyrics. But I don't think I'm crazy, so you can put that aside and not worry about me. I certainly am not nuts in the water, in the waves, surfing. I might be nuts about the water, but that's a different story.

You want proof that I'm not "non compos mentis"? That's Latin for "I can't remember my own name nor compose a coherent letter to my gal." Gal is short for Galatians. Of course, the original letters (Paul to the Galatians) are lost. The Galatians were surfers, and Paul wrote to them regarding how they should apply wax to their surfboards. But here is proof yours truly, love, Salty, is not deranged, mind not decomposing, head not unhinged, eyes right, mentally not one letter short of a full alphabet.

They had all of us talk to a shrink when we got out, during our exit physical. It's part of the discharge process, talking to an

167

Army psychiatrist. He said I was just fine, and he didn't think I'd have any trouble adjusting. He thought my period of adjustment would be a short one. A few days, he said, maybe a few weeks. Nothing to worry about. He was a handsome, confident officer who spoke in a soft, but firm, clear voice. Actually, I could barely hear him, now that I think about it. His name was Captain Torne. He asked me if I had someone waiting for me back home.

"Penina Seablouse," I told him.

He shook his head up and down, as if he had heard the name.

"You know her?" I asked.

"No, no, of course not."

He asked me a few questions about you.

"What's she like, this Penina?"

I started to describe you to him, your bubble gum hair, and the salty, downy hair on your arms, your blue eyes and freckled cheeks, and how you have to sleep with your hair over your ears because you are afraid of bugs crawling in.

"Do you have a picture?"

"No, I don't have a picture. I had one, but I lost it."

"Did you write letters to Penina, from your duty stations?"

"Yes, sir. Many."

"You are fine, Persequi. We are sending you home of

sound mind and hard body. Good luck to you and Penina."

"Thank you, Sir."

And there you have it, proof positive. Salty is of sound mind. And you know all about his hard body. So don't worry about him. But you know the person you might be concerned about, who might just be as mad as a hatter, is that batty cuckoo bird Henry Killknot, your across the alley laughing loon neighbor. Who conspires to ruin your song, hoist Salty up, and toss him into the water? Not that Sal minded being thrown into the water. You can't hurt a fish by throwing him back into the water. But Henry's flamboyance has gone overboard. And you call Salty bonkers, snookers, senseless? I am all sense but no less fishy, a board with no wave on a swelling sea, persistent Persequi, swimming to the moon,

in Love, Salvador, of Sound Mind and Hard Body.

~ ~ ~

Holy Orders

Isaac Killknot, one of Henry's little brothers, was to make his First Holy Communion, and Henry had invited us to the ceremony at the church and reception following at his parents' house. Malone and Penina did not want to go, but I wanted to see the Killknot family, Henry's brothers and sisters, and particularly his father, Joe, and I challenged Malone to come up with a good excuse not to go that would not have offended Henry, so on First Communion Sunday, Penina, Malone, and I loaded into my truck for the drive out of Refugio down Vista del Mar and around the boats at Marina del Rey and into Venice. We parked on the street in front of the church and climbed out of the truck.

"What's the good word, boys?"

Father Lynch came out of the dark shadows of the rear vestibule and crossed the sidewalk to the curb. His shadow crossed through the thin shade of the palm trees. The morning sun was still low and the shadows of the palms stretched the length of the church. We hadn't seen Father Lynch coming, and he took us all by surprise. His long thin shadow fell across the hood of the pickup truck. I knew Father Lynch from high school at Gelda.

"Surf's up, Father," I said, in response to his question.

"You don't say? Well, well," Father Lynch said, "If it isn't Salvador Persequi, home from a crusade."

"Not sure the war I was in qualified as a crusade, Father."

"No, and at any rate, I can not think of our Salvador of Gelda as a crusader, but surely you felt the weight of the cross in your struggles."

"Something like that, Father."

I introduced Penina and Malone to Father Lynch.

"And what miracle results in a visit to the Parish of Gelda from the surfers to our south?"

"We're here to see Isaac Killknot make his First Communion."

"Loads of indulgences for you all, coming to little Isaac's first communion," Lynch said, his lips stretching thin into a wide smile beneath a bulbous red nose.

"And what do you do, Mr. Malone?" Lynch asked Puck, and Puck said he was a surfer with a surf shop down in Refugio.

"Tis fine weather we live in, lads, and with the beauty of the ocean so close, but can you surf your way into heaven?"

"Surfing is heaven, Father," I said.

"And who's the lovely lass you've in tow, now, Salvador?"

"This here's a mermaid, a water-lass, Father. Penina's my

inspiration, my courtly lady."

"I see you've lost none of the sarcasm you were famous for in high school, Salvador. A war sometimes sobers a young man."

"I can't name a single soldier I knew who came out of the war sober, Father."

"Hard to follow orders when one's not sober, I should think. But of what court is Penina a lady?"

"Good question. She holds her own court, the court of hip beat post existentialism she's been calling it lately."

Father Lynch leaned in with his big, red nose sagging beneath his beady green eyes and stared at Penina and turned back toward me. He was going to say something, but just then Isaac and Henry pulled up, and Isaac jumped out of Henry's car and ran over to me and wrapped his arms around me for a welcome home hug. I had not seen any of Henry's brothers or sisters or his parents yet, but I liked them all, and was looking forward to the reception at the Killknot's place after church.

"Welcome home, Salty," Isaac said, retreating from the hug and falling in with Henry.

We had arrived at the church a bit early, but the curb was quickly filling up with cars now, parishioners. Little girls in long billowing white dresses climbed out of sedans, blue rosary beads in their hands, white lace doily hats pinned to their heads with glossy black bobby pins, and boys in starched white shirts tucked tightly into salt and pepper corduroy pants scuffled up the sidewalk and sidled into the church.

"You better be going in and getting into your cassock now, Isaac," Henry said.

"Thanks for the ride," Henry.

"See you later, Ike," Henry said. "No falling asleep on the altar again this morning. He'll be taking back some of those indulgences you've earned this week."

Father Lynch took us all in with a twisted grin and bowing slightly flapped his black gown around and strode off to greet some parishioners.

"What was that?" Penina said.

"Don't worry. I'll protect you," I said.

"That was so weird the way he leaned into my face. I think I smelled alcohol on his breath."

"No doubt. He probably uses it for after-shave lotion," I said.

"Indeed," Henry added, "brushes his teeth and gargles with it."

We went into the church. The children were lining up

against the back wall of the narthex. The thick, waxy smell of the burning votive candles mixed with the light, soapy perfume coming from the girls. The children were leaving a trail of salty sand across the polished floor. We went into the nave, and I was hit with the cool, dark, incensed air of the big, empty church. I couldn't remember the last time I was in a church. There was something slightly intoxicating about the air, sunlight filtering through the high windows, flickering on rising shafts of dust.

Henry motioned to us to go into one of the rear pews on the epistle side of the church, but when we all got seated, Henry did not whisper. He sat at the end of the pew near the aisle, his arm over the pew back and around Penina. I sat between Penina and Malone.

"Isaac's been getting up at four in the morning all week to serve at the early morning mass, and I've been giving him rides and teaching him to surf in the afternoons," Henry said. "I've never been so tired. Neither has Isaac. He fell asleep on the porch outside the sacristy one morning waiting for Father Lynch to come over and open up the church. Then he fell asleep again on his knees, kneeling at the altar." Henry was quietly laughing. "I wish you could have seen it, Sal," Henry said. "Old Father Lynch snapping his fingers behind his back. Isaac woke up with a start and reached for the bells and started shaking them. But it wasn't time for the bells. Lynch waved him over to the credence table. It was time for the wine and water, to wash the holy man's fingers in the water and pour and drink some of the wine. You should have been there, Sal. The ringing of the bells out of place shook up some of the old folks in the front pews, and Ike later said he caught the fierce eyes of Sister Columnquill on him when he was coming back from the credence table."

"I remember Sister Columnquill," I whispered.

"It didn't look like she was praying for me, Ike said," Henry said. "And old Mrs. Miller, bent and twisted like an oak tree from her arthritis, and dry and rotting and bent over near to the floor from her twelfth kid, was struggling to stand up, but Sister Columnquill was up and helping her back down. Miller must have thought it was time to come up to communion. It was Ike's bells out of place set her off," Henry said, laughing with an exaggerated wickedness.

"Were you there?" I asked Henry.

"Ah, I sort of came and went, trying to keep an eye out for Isaac. You know I don't trust that bastard Lynch."

"Is Father Lynch not to be trusted?"

"Father, you say? I'd sooner be orphaned lame and blind in the Black Hole of Calcutta than call that pustule headed Lynch my father," Henry said.

"I'm not sure the Black Hole was an orphanage," I said.

"You should see the church for weekday morning mass," Henry said. "The place is empty, the back of the church dark and empty, full of dark shadows, a few scattered bodies in the front pews, old people, a couple of nuns, sometimes a high school kid from Gelda probably performing a penance, and old man Lynch up there starting his drinking day off with a strong dose of the musty blood of Christ."

Father Lynch held the small white host of the ecclesiastical bread high over his head, in the tips of his fingers, like a guitar pick, his back to the church, now full of anxious families and friends of the First Communicants. The children had walked in procession up the aisle, genuflecting to sounds of a metal cricket fingered by Sister Columnquill. After the church had filled, Father Lynch had indicated he was ready to begin the ceremony, and the altar boys had led the way forward, the girls on the epistle side and the boys on the gospel side of the nave. As the children were slowly moving up the aisle, the sun came striking through the stained glass windows above the choir loft and shot across the dusty air and caught the statue of the virgin Mary in the heart, and I heard Isaac ringing the bells and heard a long slinky surf guitar riff in my head.

"There's no money for the altar boys in the early morning mass," Henry whispered to us. "The church gives me the fantods, anymore, but there's money in weddings and funerals, more in weddings than funerals. Nobody likes a funeral, but Ike should make something for this morning's service, if Lynch doesn't steal it all. You guys coming to the reception at my folks' place?" Henry asked, looking at me.

"Yes, of course," I said, and Henry shook his head up and down, looking pleased.

An old lady in the pew in front of us turned around and glared and put her finger across her lips to silence me. I looked helplessly at Henry, and he made a sign of the cross ending with a kiss he blew toward her. She turned back around, shaking her head, and Henry looked at me with a big, childish smile on his face, and ran his fingers into Penina's stomach, taking her by surprise and tickling her. She doubled up and knocked the back of the pew in front of us with her knees. Henry had trouble stifling his laughter, and Penina socked him in his arm. I looked at Malone. He was looking straight ahead, either enraptured or in a bored daze. I couldn't tell which. I could smell Penina sitting next to me and feel her arm and leg against mine. I put my arm around her. She had moved closer to me trying to get away from the mischievous Henry. I thought of Penina rising on a beam of lighted dust toward the high ceiling and remembered how peaceful a church might be for a few moments.

The service finally ended and the children scooted back down the center aisle and spilled out into the outside vestibule, and as soon as they went out the church doors and into the entryway, they buzzed like cicadas. They were happy to have the ceremony consummated. They talked about the host, what it tasted like. Did someone chew it, a sin, or did Father Lynch's dry, scaly fingers touch anyone's lips? The girls shook their heads and made faces. Then the families separated the children and cameras popped out, and Father Lynch and Sister Columnquill politely posed with family after family with their First Communicants.

"Let's beat this scene," Henry said. "By the time the day's over, all the little buggers will be needing to go to confession again."

We drove over to the Killknot's house, stopping at a liquor store on the way to pick up some beer. Henry said his dad had a couple of coolers full of beer buried in ice, but he didn't want to run out. When we got to the Killknot place, we had to park a block away. It looked like the entire parish had crashed little Isaac's reception. The front yard, the front porch, the house, the back porch, and the back yard were filling fast with First Communicants and their families. Some of the smaller children were running around the yard playing a game of capture the flag. Henry enlisted a couple of his younger brothers to help ice the beer reinforcement, and Malone, Penina, and I made our way through the front door and through the living room into the kitchen, where we found Joe Killknot, Henry's father.

"Ge-ge-get Sal-Sal-Salty and Pu-Pu-Puck a beer, will you, Icky?" Joe Killknot said. "How the he-he-hell are you, Salty? I'll go-go-go to hell riding a shovel. I'm ha-ha-happy as a ba-ba-backyard hog to see you," and he pulled me close for a hug, and I could smell the gunk coming out of his ears.

"Hi, Joe," I said close to his ear as he hugged me. His clothes smelled like wet pipes.

A big gob of goop ran out of his ear and down his neck. He pulled out a snot green, soiled handkerchief and wiped his neck and ear and ran a finger into his ear with the handkerchief and cleaned it out.

"My go-god damn ears be-be-been acting up again. Hello, Puck. How the hell are you, son?"

"Good, sir. Nice to see you again," Puck said.

"What's that? You'll ha-ha-have to speak up, Pu-Puck. I'm a little hard on hearing, you know."

"Doing great! Surf's up and I made it through church!"

179

Malone yelled so loud the windows rattled.

"Oh, I see, I see," Joe said, shaking his head up and down. "I see, yes. We'll, you be sure and tell him I sa-sa-said hi, now. Wi-wi-will you do that for me?"

Malone gave me a stupefied look.

"Just say yes," I said. "He didn't understand you."

"Yes!" Malone yelled.

"He ain't that hard of hearing, Puck," Henry said, coming into the kitchen. "Trick is, you have to look at him when you talk, so he can read your lips. If you talk too loud, if you yell, somehow he can't make sense of what you're saying."

"Yeah, yeah, I see what you mean," Henry's father said.

"Where's Mom?" Henry asked his father.

"She's in and out setting up the backyard. Sarah will be real glad to see you all, too, Salty," Joe said, smoothly this time.

The kitchen was full of people coming and going. Out on the back porch a couple of coolers kept opening and closing.

"Do I know this pretty girl?" Joe asked, again without a stutter, looking at Penina.

"I'm Penina Seablouse," Penina loudly proclaimed, holding out her hand.

"Glad to meet you, Pe-pe-pina. You all st-stay and get something to eat now. You hear me?"

Isaac was back from the cooler with the beers. He took a long swig off mine, behind his father's back, before handing it to me with a smile. He handed beers to Puck and to his father.

"You get Pe-Pina a beer?"

Isaac went back out to the coolers on the porch.

Henry's sister Marina came into the kitchen. She was my age, and we had been friends at Gelda. When we were freshmen, we once rode in the back of the school bus to a football game, and I had tried, unsuccessfully, to give her a kiss.

"Hi, Salty," Marina said, glancing at Penina and looking back at me. There was an awkward pause, and Marina and I hugged.

"Your hair's so short."

"Yeah. I'm letting it grow now, though."

"I saved all your letters," Marina said, and, after a short pause, "all two of them."

"Oh, yeah. Guess I'm not much of a letter writer," I said.

"That's not what Henry said."

"Why don't we go out back where's there's more room?" Henry said. "Nothing like a wedding or a funeral or a sacrament to bring out the catholic in the Catholic families. This is the beauty of the church of sacraments. The saints will always go marching in, Lord, Lord, and how I do want to be in that number."

We followed Henry's lead out the kitchen door onto the back porch and down the steps into the yard. On the porch we said hello to Sarah, Henry's mother. She was a short, wiry woman, bony and skinny, with sharp looks out of hazel eyes. She smiled at Penina and asked her if she put color in her hair to make it go that kind of greenish yellow. Henry started to laugh and his mother gave him a sharp elbow to the ribs.

Penina and I sat in a circle of folding chairs under a shady oak tree in the backyard. Malone had run off, but he was somewhere in the house. The Killknots had set up a hodgepodge of tables with benches and chairs around the yard. A long, folding table had been set up against the back porch, and women had been filling it with covered potluck dishes. Someone came into the yard with a big cake decorated with a rosary made of frosting. The cake went into the kitchen, a squad of kids following. Pitchers of water and punch and a coffee jug with glasses and mugs filled a card table set up at the end of the folding table. The chairs in our circle filled up with Henry's older brothers and sisters. The Killknot children all wanted to say hi to me. I remembered the large family besieged by the daily vicissitudes of working class life on the border of poverty. The little kids quickly scooted off after Ike bugged me until I showed the scar. The older children wanted to talk to Henry.

"Dad got laid off again," Marina said to Henry.

"I didn't even know he'd been working," Henry said.

"You don't get around much, anymore," Marina said.

Across the yard Isaac started yelling at Stan, one of his younger brothers.

"Mind your own beeswax, why don't you?"

"Mom told you not to take such big sips from the beers. I'm telling."

"Isaac! Bring Dad that beer, will you now?" Joe called from the back porch, referring to himself in the third person, and suddenly, rising above the din of still incoming families and friends, there were Killknot yells crisscrossing around the house and yard, like some nefarious cat on the prowl for trouble had aroused a bevy of birds from a nested nap.

"Georgie! David wants you," Isabel yelled from an upstairs open window.

"Mom! Mary won't stop bugging me and Dilly."

"Mary, have you finished wrapping the forks in napkins?"

"Mom, no one cares, for Christ sake."

Whack!

"I ought to wash your mouth out with soap, you yelling the Lord's name in vain like that all around my house, with us expecting Father Lynch and Sister Columnquill any minute now. I swun. Some people are just so selfish." This was the voice of Sarah Killknot, Henry's long-suffering, non-surfing mother.

"You ki-ki-kids stop all that god damn yelling, will you?" Joe yelled from the kitchen. "God damn it, anyhow."

"Isaac, you bring those trashcans back in the yard?"

"Yeah."

"Why didn't you put them in the garage like I asked?"

"Paul just hauled a bunch of surfboard stuff in there. They're all making new boards."

"I want you to go he-help me over to Bernie's tomorrow. I got la-laid off again. We got to lo-lo-load up with the lead and pot. I go-got to get them ditches back covered up before the co-concrete comes."

"Okay, Dad."

"Get these bo-boys another be-beer, will you, Marina?" Joe said, coming down the back porch steps to join us.

"Dad, they can get their own beers," Marina said.

"I swun," Henry's mother said, coming down the back porch. "I hate it when people do me like that," she said, walking through the yard, talking to herself.

"You kids he-help your mother now," Joe called out, addressing himself to a general audience, but to no one in particular, and so his order appeared to go unheeded.

Joe came over and sat down next to me. His clothes were soiled, and he smelled like cooled lead. A coagulated drop of green snot hung from each of his ear lobes.

"Old Sarah, she don't wa-walk like she used to, Salty. Then again, neither do I."

Empty beer cans started to pile up. Some of the children were growing fussy. The backyard tables were full of children and parents and friends talking, coming and going to and from the house, voices swirling around the house and yard like little water eddies, children laughing, screaming, crying, a mom yelling here, a father cussing there, more beer brought out to refill the coolers, and Sarah yelled it was time to eat, and a food line started up at the long folding table, now full of plates and bowls and pitchers.

Penina and I waited until the line shortened. We got plates and started to move down the long table. There were bowls filled with green salad, potato salad, noodle salad, three bean salad with red peppers swimming in red wine vinegar, fruit salad. A few bowls of chips had already been emptied, and Sarah sent Ike for more. A big platter of ham and roast beef filled the center of the table. A giant bowl of deviled eggs, sprinkled with paprika, attracted a slow moving, fattened horse fly. A bowl of pork and beans looked good, full of fatty bacon chunks. Penina grabbed my hand as I dug deep into the beans, but let go, laughing, running her hand through her hair. There was a bowl of fried chicken legs and wings and another of barbecued chicken breasts and thighs, a couple of yellow jackets hovering above a fat, juicy-looking breast. There was a big pile of something that looked like lasagna, and a very fancy plate filled with neatly packed rows of what might have been grape leaves stuffed with something, rice and pine nuts, Penina guessed. There was a plate of hot dogs and another of beer sausages and another of rolls and buns. At the end of the long food table, we came to the card table full of drinks. There was a gallon of milk, a pitcher of water and another of punch, and gallon jugs of cheap wine, one white, and one red, next to short stacks of red, white, and blue plastic cups.

Everyone was seated somewhere, at a table or on at step or on the grass, eating, talking, drinking, when Father Lynch and Sister Columnquill arrived, and Sarah Killknot announced that Father Lynch would say grace. He did, keeping the blessing mercifully short, and Lynch and Columnquill took seats next to Sarah and Joe Killknot, and at Sarah's instructions a couple of the Killknot kids went to the long table and filled plates and glasses and served the clergy.

Folks ate and talked and drank, went back to the long table for seconds and thirds, told stories and jokes and on seconds and thirds started repeating the stories and jokes, emptied the wine jugs, filled a couple of garbage cans with empty beer cans, the food on the long table dwindling, plates picked cleaned, bowls emptied. Finally, the feast seemed close to an end, and the First Holy Communicant reception was treated to a few folk songs played by a trio of young Killknot guitarists, while Aqua and Marina Killknot brought out the huge cake decorated with the blue rosary beads.

The party went on, and a fresh coffee urn was set up next to the cake. Sarah Killknot announced we would all take a break from eating while the kids gathered up dirty plates and glasses before the cake benediction and desert. Guests began to stand and stretch and visit with friends from other tables. Long lines formed at both of the Killknot bathrooms. A couple of elders slipped down in their chairs and were soon breathing through their mouths, snoring a bit. Even the children seemed naturally to be slowing down, and for a few minutes the yard was quiet and peaceful as folks sat with their thoughts without moving or talking much. I might have dozed off myself for a few minutes.

I got up from my chair and stretched. A few of the older

kids were in the garage, at the rear of the lot, and I walked back to the garage, which was shaded, and joined them while Penina helped with the clearing of the dirty dishes. Lucas Crux and John Humulus had arrived, and Lucas came out to the garage carrying beers. Henry's sister Aqua was there, apparently hiding from kitchen duties, and opened the beers and handed them around.

Humulus had been hit in the head the day before with a surfboard, and had fresh stitches between his eyes.

"Lucky he didn't get knocked out cold, probably would have drowned," Lucas said.

"Lucky his nose didn't break. Skin all busted open though," Henry said.

"Let's see," Aqua said, and Humulus pulled the bandage off his forehead.

"Wow," Aqua said. "What happened?"

"I went over the falls," Humulus said.

"You pearled," Lucas said.

"I went over the falls."

"His board pearled and shot back up into his face," Lucas said.

"I was going over the falls in a pile of white water."

"Did you pass out?" Henry asked.

"I just saw white, but I don't think I passed out."

"He came up, and you know what water does to blood on your face? I thought he was dead," Lucas said. "I thought his face had exploded or something crazy. I thought he was dead."

"It's not so bad. I'd leave the bandage off, though," Aqua said. "Let it get some air. Have a little scar, be sexy," Aqua said.

"Aren't you a little young to be talking like that?" Humulus said.

I went out of the garage to find Penina and to help with the cleanup. She was in the yard, wiping the tables and chairs down and folding the chairs. Most of the folding chairs had been borrowed from the church hall.

"Sarah wants to know can you take the chairs back to the church in your truck," Penina said.

"Sure, I said. Where's Malone?"

"I saw him going upstairs with Marina."

We heard Sarah yelling from the kitchen. "I mean clean, really clean!"

"Who's she yelling at now," I asked.

"Dilly and Maggie, I think. It's their day to do dishes, apparently. Rotten deal, they've been complaining, dishwashing duty falling on the day of the big reception. But I've never heard a family that yells so much."

"Put some elbow grease in it!" Sarah yelled in the kitchen. "That's an order!"

"Yeah, I don't know. Maybe it has something to do with Joe's hearing problem."

"Get Dad a beer, will ya, Itchy?" we heard Joe Killknot's voice coming from the kitchen, and Isaac came out to the back porch and grabbed a cool one from the ice box, opened it with the church key, and was drowning down a good bit of it, what appeared to be beyond the legal sip, when his dad came out and grabbed the beer out of his hand.

Joe gave Isaac the Killknot-famous curled lip and said, "Not that much elbow grease," the curled lip curling into a crooked smile.

The Killknot kids were all put to work cleaning up. Soon, most of the families had packed up and gone home. Sarah wanted to get the chairs back to the church, so Henry, Malone, Humulus, and Crux all helped load the chairs into my truck. Aqua wanted to go for a ride in the truck, so Crux and I with Aqua took the chairs back over to the church hall, unpacked them, and drove back to the Killknot's place.

We were gone maybe an hour or so. When we got back, I found Penina sitting with Malone in the Killknot's back yard.

"What's up?" I said

"Just another solid gold weekend in sunny Southern California," Puck said. But he wasn't wearing his usual sunny look. Shadows had fallen across the yard. "What's wrong?" I said.

Henry was sitting on the ground under the tree with his head down on his knees.

"What's the matter, Isaac?" I said. "What happened?"

"Mom was spanking Isabel silly, and Isabel was screaming bloody murder," Isaac said.

"What did I do? Isabel was yelling," Marina put in. "Isabel was getting to that point where she couldn't breathe. She tried to hold her hands behind her to catch the whacks, but that just made mom that much madder. 'It's not what you did, it's what you didn't do,' Mom yelled."

"It's one of her favorite things to say," Isaac said.

"'I'm sorry, Mom! I'm sorry!' We heard Isabel yelling," Marina said.

"'Sorry! Sorry! What's sorry got to do with it!' Whack! Whack! Whack! 'And stop that crying before I give you something to cry about,' Mom said," Isaac said.

"Another one of her favorite sayings," Marina said.

"Henry came running in and grabbed Mom's hands and twisted her arms back and started yelling at her to stop," Isaac said.

"And Mom slapped Henry across the face," Marina said.

"And Henry went running outside, and there he is," Isaac said. "And he won't look up or talk to nobody."

"And Mom was all mad because Henry beat up Father Lynch," Marina said.

"What?"

Suddenly Henry got up from where he was sitting and ran out of the yard, tears streaming down his face, his hands clinched, his face as red as blood-dark grapes.

"What the hell?" I looked at Malone and Penina.

"Henry had the priest by the neck, squeezing," Malone said.

"Father Lynch?"

"Yeah. I thought he was a goner. Henry had him by the throat and was yelling in his face. Henry told him he was supposed to help the family, help raise the kids, and he slammed him against the door, three times, Lynch's head bouncing off the door like a paddleball. The nun was screaming and yelling at Henry, but I couldn't get Henry to let go. He was a madman."

"Where was Henry's dad?"

"Sleeping on the living room couch," Isaac said.

"He wasn't sleeping," Marina said.

"Jesus."

"Yeah.

"Where was your mom?"

"She was on Henry too, trying to pull him away from Lynch."

"'What am I supposed to do, perform a fucking miracle here?' Father Lynch said," Marina said, "and that set Henry to laughing. Then he started shaking and crying, and he ran outside here where you found him sitting, and Father Lynch said something about how he had orders to do what he did, holy orders, he said," Marina said.

We heard the scrunch-screech sound of gears shifting and tires spinning on asphalt and heard Henry's souped-up Corvette speed past out front and down the street.

"All this while I'm taking the chairs back?"

"Yeah," Malone said.

Penina hadn't said anything, but she was looking at me as if she expected me to do something, solve something.

"Where did all this happen?"

"Upstairs, outside Isaac's room."

Everyone looked at Isaac.

"Well, I didn't do anything wrong," Isaac said. "Father Lynch said he wanted to look at my baseball cards."

"Where were you, Puck?"

"Next door in Marina's room."

"What?"

"Marina wanted to show me her shells."

"Jesus, Puck."

"Hey, man, Marina's right here."

Everyone looked at Marina, and she looked away, her face reddening.

"Where's Joe and Sarah now?"

"Joe woke up dazed," Malone said. "He told us all to go outside and took Sarah into their bedroom. It's been quiet since, and you came back, and Henry took off, but you saw and heard that."

The noise of an explosion near or far comes as a surprise. Explosions are not like thunder. We feel impending thunder with the other animals in the vicinity. But later, Penina would say her cat, Castus, had been acting strange, jumping up onto the bed. But Castus's odd behavior might have been explained by my sleeping with Penina, which the cat found strange. I thought I had heard a chain of sounds rushing by, like a train, the ground shaking. There was a blast, the ignition of the fuel, and the noise kept coming, the sounds of things breaking and tearing, pulling apart, the sound of

194

debris landing, a blending of glass, boards, and wires, and the smoldering sounds and echoes of the original blast, and finally all I could hear was the ringing in the ears. But someone was screaming or yelling. I had covered Penina, the blast seeming to come through her wall. Castus had scampered under the bed.

Penina and I had been asleep. The blast came just before dawn. A shattering, scattering crack awoke us, and Henry Killknot's front door came flying across Penina's deck and crashed through the window of Penina's apartment. Explosions seem sudden, but they are often the result of a series of mishaps, mistakes, false steps. An explosion produces a shock wave that is full of innuendo. Heard from a great distance, the explosion comes as a whisper, a rumor. Up close, one is implicated, defamed, smeared. One wishes for a drink, a sprinkling of holy water.

I grabbed Penina's phone off the nightstand and dialed the operator to get fire and rescue, implicating her as well. Everyone plays a role in the explosion scenario. And anyone who didn't see the flash or hear the boom would get the story soon enough and would have the chance of joining the murmuring audience repeating rumors like reciting beads on a rosary. They could read the story in the local newspaper, read quotes by those who were near, look at the photographs, identify and recognize and speculate and talk.

I didn't yet understand what had happened, but there was a door sticking through Penina's window that had been preceded by a blast from across the way, and we had heard screams. We rushed out of Penina's apartment and from the deck saw Henry come staggering naked from his apartment across the alley. He got to the middle of the alley and sat down.

"Jesus, Henry," I yelled down into the street. Across the alley, his apartment was misshapen and smoldering. Dust and debris still fell, confetti and smoke circling in the air.

"Henry, come up here," Penina said.

Henry looked up but shook his head, slightly, side to side, indicating no.

Penina ran into her apartment and came back with my shirt and ran down and held it out to Henry, still sitting in the middle of the alley, his legs drawn up, his arms on his knees. I followed her down. The skin on his shoulders was curling. His hair was singed and he smelled of burnt hair. He looked up at me. His face looked like it had been severely sunburned. His eyebrows were singed. I knelt down next to him, and Penina handed me the shirt, but Henry shook his head, no. An El Segundo police car skidded to a halt and a cop came running up, unsure of what to do, looking this way and that, hesitating. Then came the firemen, absurdly dressed for snow. The alley filled with people emptying out of houses and apartments. The paramedics put a white sheet over Henry's shoulders and back and doused him with a clear liquid. They loaded him into an ambulance and drove off. Henry ended up in the burn ward at Los Angeles General. We went back into Penina's place, and she rescued Castus from under the bed. We went back out, Castus in Penina's arms, and we walked through the crowd and started up the hill toward Puck's place, ignoring questions of what had happened. Puck came running down the hill and found us and turned and walked with us. No one said a word. In the street, strange, light confetti had fallen. We were half way up the hill, but still we saw pages strewn about the street, fallen with the residue from the blast. Two sheets of paper had fallen in my path. I was about to step on them. I saw cursive handwriting and a drawing. I bent down and picked up the pages. They were Penina's letters, the originals, from the box at Puck's party, the box I had thrown off the Refugio jetty. I had noticed the white paper falling in the alley moments after the blast, drifting down through the light morning fog, flicking about like playful, pecking, white pigeons.

Henry had blown out the flame of the pilot light on his stove and turned the gas burners on, leaving the door to the oven open. He had done the same with the built in gas wall heater. A shard of broken glass shell held together by the label from a bottle of whiskey suggested that he thought he might ensure he didn't wake up before the gas finished him off. But the gas proved not enough, and early in the morning, dazed and groggy from gas and whiskey, he awoke and got out of bed and lit a cigarette. He had second and third degree flash burns over seventy-five percent of his body.

That evening, we went to the hospital to visit him. He was sedated but awake and still probably in shock. He said he was thirsty and wanted a milkshake. The nurse said we could bring him one. I volunteered to go get him a milkshake, glad to get out of the hospital and the smell of the burn ward, leaving Henry with Penina and Malone.

I got back with the milkshake. Henry wanted to know if he'd be able to go back to his apartment. Malone tried to explain how the roof had lifted off, the door flying through Penina's window, but Penina said we shouldn't talk about it now. A nurse came in and said Henry should limit visitors to two at a time, and I volunteered to leave. I said goodbye to Henry and went back down to the lobby to wait for Malone and Penina.

At Henry's funeral, the Killknot family all squeezed into the front pew, Sarah, Joe, Marina, Aqua, and all the rest of kids.

Isaac joined them, his head down. He would not be serving as an altar boy at Henry's funeral mass. Joe was wearing a tie I recognized as one of Henry's, one of a new batch Henry had recently purchased to wear to his law office job.

Father Lynch performed the funeral mass slowly and deliberately, dressed in glossy, flowing black vestments. There had been no discussion, apparently, regarding Henry possibly not receiving the last sacrament because he might have been a suicide. He had lasted three days in the burn ward before he died from infection in his vital organs. Father Lynch may have had several reasons for his immediate, local dispensation. The casket was kept closed. In his sermon, Lynch mentioned Vatican II, mercy, and tolerance. Still, he also mentioned something about holy orders, almost suggesting Henry had been on a holy, short leash. None of it made much sense, but I was having trouble concentrating. The church at Henry's funeral, unlike the church at Isaac's First Communion, though it was the same church, felt suffocating. The burning incense reminded me of Henry in the burn ward.

After the funeral, Isaac came up to me, and we hugged without words, but then he asked me, "Salty, is Henry going to go to hell?"

"No, Isaac. I don't think so."

"But Aqua said Henry killed himself, and Sister

Columnquill said that when people kill themselves they go straight to hell and never even have a chance for purgatory." Water was filling Isaac's eyes. "She said they got a special place for them down there, a special circle, she said, in hell, for the people that do suicide."

"No, Isaac. I don't think hell is laid out like that. It couldn't possibly be so neat and orderly as having circles. But anyway, Henry did not kill himself. It was an accident."

"But why did Henry kill himself?"

"Henry did not kill himself, Isaac. It probably would have been a good idea for Henry to have talked to someone, but I know he wanted to live, and he was just having trouble figuring out how to live, that's all. It was all an accident. He didn't realize his place was all full of gas."

"You think Henry's in hell, Salty?"

"Hell is an ocean with no waves, Isaac, and I'll bet Henry's got plenty of good waves now, all to himself. Okay?"

"Okay, Salty, if you say so."

"I do say so, and if anyone tries to tell you any different, I want you to send them to me. Will you do that?"

"Yes, Salty. I will. I don't want Henry to be in hell, Salty. I want him to be able to surf."

"Look, Isaac, you don't have to believe in that hell. Hell is what we create for ourselves in this life by not reading the waves right, and we get caught inside. That's what happened to Henry. Father Lynch's hell does not exist. You don't have to worry about going to hell after you die. That's all a wrong story, a bad myth."

"I know that, Salty. Henry told me all that. And I don't believe in hell."

"Then why are you so worried that Henry might be in hell?"

"Because Father Lynch said the first people the devil comes after are the ones who don't believe in him. Do you think the devil came after Henry, Salty?"

We suddenly found ourselves back in the Killknot's backyard, the same tables and chairs set out, the same coolers full of beer on the back porch, the same kids running around the yard, their parents sitting at tables, eating and drinking, though no one seemed quite as free and easy as they had been at the First Communion reception, and neither Father Lynch nor Sister Columnquill came by to visit the family. I drove the chairs back to the church hall again, this time Puck and Marina driving over with me. On the way back from the church, Malone pointed out a building he was bidding on to start up another surf shop in Venice. We got back to the Killknot's, where the sadness in the yard was like a thick fog. Joe Killknot looked years older, walked with a stoop, like he had thrown his back out, and Sarah Killknot sat alone, up on the back porch, neither raising her voice nor talking to anyone. The Killknot kids were all on their best behavior. Humulus and Crux came by again, but no one else from Henry's days at Gelda dropped by, and no one from UCLA. A couple of middle aged men dressed in suits, apparently from Henry's law office on Wilshire Boulevard, came to the funeral and stopped by the house afterward. One of them handed Joe Killknot a large envelope and they both gave Joe their business cards. Lynch had said the mass of the dead, but funerals are for the living.

We drove back to Refugio. Penina and I were both living temporarily in my room above Puck's surf shop, Penina still insisting we sleep head to toe. It would be a week or longer before Penina's apartment could be repaired. When we got home, Puck and I stayed downstairs in the shop to drink a beer and plan out the week ahead, and Penina went upstairs to check on Castus. The cat was acting strange again, Penina explained. She didn't like having to move to a new place.

"Salty, you're not planning anything stupid like Henry there, are you?" Puck asked me, after Penina had left us to go upstairs.

"Why would you ask me that?"

"I don't know, man. Just seems like a lot of crazy stuff going down since you got back home."

"Well, Puck, thanks for asking, but I'll be okay."

"You let me know if you need anything, Salty," Puck said, and he patted me on the shoulder.

Puck and I drank a couple more beers and talked about the week ahead and the future of the surf shop, and by the time I went upstairs, Penina and Castus were both in bed, sound asleep. I sat down at my little table and wrote Penina another letter.

Dear Penina:

It wasn't so easy talking to Henry's father as it was to Isaac. Isaac seemed relieved to know that I didn't think Henry was in hell, but "Why did Henry do this?" Joe Killknot asked me, more concerned than Isaac with Henry's past than his future. What could I say? Aqua and Marina were standing on either side of Mr. Killknot, as if he might fall.

"I don't know, Joe," I said. "I don't understand it any better than you do."

"But you were He-Henry's be-be-best friend," Mr. Killknot said. "You and Henry were like brothers," Joe said, with no stutter. "Henry believed in Jesus. Didn't he?"

What could I say? That Henry was a hater? That Henry

hated his life? That Henry hated his mother and his brothers and sisters and you, too, Joe, most of all, you? And even if I could have said that, how do I know it was true? People are more complicated than simple explanations like that. Henry loved his family, loved his mother and father. I know − it's an odd way to show love, a strange way to reach out. Did he get drunk then turn the gas on? Or did he turn the gas on then got drunk? Did he not stop to think that he was blowing up the block, the alleyway, and that he might hurt others in addition to himself? He had to have been drunk already, and wasn't thinking clearly. If only there had been some break in the chain of events. I had looked over at this place before going in for the night. I had noticed the lights off, the windows darkened. I could have gone over to say hello and drink a beer. Instead, I wanted to go inside and be with you. Was I his best friend, as his father said? Was I any kind of friend?

Where is Henry now? Am I my brother's keeper? Bubo watched out for me, and I watched out for Bubo. Bubo and I were not brothers. We were buddies in a system. We learned to be both independent and to watch out for one another. Why could Henry not take care of himself?

Jesus said to follow him, not that he was going anywhere, town to town, on the make. What was I supposed to tell Isaac? That Jesus said to leave your family, forget where you come from, leave your home? No, that isn't quite right, not what he meant at all. Don't be anxious over your parents, where your home is, where you come from. Jesus said it does not matter who your parents are, what tribe claims you. This is something war teaches, maybe, if it teaches anything, which of course it does not.

Jesus wanted us to be free. The only place I have ever felt free is on the water. War is absolute shame. Jesus taught that we have nothing to be ashamed of, not of our parents, not of our home. Why was Henry so full of shame? What did he expect? Henry had not figured out how to free himself of his shame. If it doesn't matter who our parents are, does it follow that it doesn't matter who our children are?

You look so peaceful, sleeping, Castus curled up at your side. I've decided to paddle out and live on the water. I'll be leaving tomorrow evening. There are some things I should finish in the shop before paddling out. Don't say anything to Puck. I'll explain it to him. There's no problem. I do regret the letters, the ones I wrote to you, and Henry's bizarre behavior with them, and I do wish you had those letters back, but I also regret the letters you wrote to me, that I did not save them. I should have been a better listener.

Anyway, I think I'd like a few days alone, now that I'm back, a few days to adjust to the adjustment period, the reentry. I'll

205

paddle out, live on the water for a few days, and paddle back in, a second homecoming. I figure I should be able to live on the water for at least three days and nights, maybe longer. We'll see.

Love, Salty

~ ~ ~

On a Surfboard in Santa Monica Bay

In the middle of the night, I awoke to water slapping with life bubbling to the surface under a vast, purple darkness, warm air rising in a mist, curling and drifting and disappearing into the night sky. I never felt alone on the ocean. I always felt as if something was watching me, something under my surfboard, nearby, in the water with me, or beneath me, some angel of the surf, some animal from the deep. When I first paddled out, I paused just beyond the break and looked back at the beach, and Penina was still watching me. A sea lion popped up, a couple of yards away from me, its wet head like a dog's head. The sea lion sank back underwater. Then it popped up again on the other side of me, its brown agate eyes watching me, its skin slick and sleek, looking tough and thick and covered with a wet film, its hair and whiskers wet and shiny, its small ears brushed back. I wondered what sea lions hear under water.

I left at sunset, the waves emptying out for the day, the distant light a stone washed orange wall, nothing on the horizon. The waves emitted deep creaking tones that evening, sea toads belching love calls. I looked like any ordinary surfer paddling out, but once past the break, I kept going. The waves were cylindrical that night, hollow, breaking deep, sonorously. I heard deep bass notes and kick bass drums as I paddled out and rolled my surfboard under a few breaking tubes, pipes with the texture of rough green bubbled glass.

I had said goodbye to Penina, who had walked down to the water with me, and stuck a bar of surfboard wax into the back pocket of my swim trunks. I would have paddled out naked, I told her, but I didn't want to be mistaken for a kook. That's all I carried with me, the bar of wax in my trunks. I think Penina thought I was joking.

"You can't live on the water," she said. "You'll die of hypothermia. You'll starve. You'll be eaten by sharks."

"Nonsense. I'll be fine. You're taking this far too literally."

"Your legs will get literally cold."

"I'll get used to it."

"I love you, Sal."

"I love you, too, Penina, oceanically."

"Don't act crazy, Sal, please?"

I slipped silently into the shell of the bay, slithering under the waves curling like whelks sliding over me.

Behind me, Penina grew smaller and smaller, and El Porto shrank, while I grew larger the farther out I paddled. By the time I reached the middle of the bay, Los Angeles was as small as a snail, a screed of electric light combing across the basin. I could see the lights of the beachfront houses and apartments at Venice, the dwellings atop the cliffs above Sunset, the princely Palisades lit with colorful landscape lights, the blue pool at the Malibu Getty just north of the small Sunset point, the perpendicular piers (Malibu, Santa Monica, Venice, the Standard Oil double pier between El Segundo and El Porto, Manhattan, Hermosa, the horseshoe pier at Redondo), the splashing shadows of the Palos Verdes cliffs and Catalina Island. And I could still see Penina, now cloaked in a white shawl, walking up the beach with the grieving Donna Jabanoso. Angel and Peggy Ann were coming down the steps from the Strand to meet them. I did not see Puck.

There's nothing like being in the water in the evening when the sun comes so close. I listened to the waves. Sound travels like skipping stones across water. I could hear the airplanes taking off and landing at the airport, the sounds the jets made scraping against the landscape. Once out over the water, their engines opened full to breathe huge gulps of rushing air, the engines shrilly screamed. The screaming from the jets penetrated the water the distance of light. Late at night, quiet oil tankers slipped into the bay like strange whales, the mournful moans of their deep horns sounding like bass saxophones blowing under water. In the morning a silent color came across the sky, heralding the approaching orange light as the sun floated over the tops of the distant peaks and white light drooped like willow branches and shot like water sprouts through the canyons, filling the Los Angles basin.

The bay smelled salty, oily, and fishy. I was hungry and went ashore at the Palos Verdes Cove, north of Haggerty's, and leaving my board up on the rocky beach, I swam out into the cove, drifting east to the inside rocks and kelp beds, and dove for abalone. I caught none. I needed a snorkel and mask if I was going to survive on skin diving. I ended up eating some fairly good-sized sand crabs I caught with my hands in a sandy pool at the edge of the water. After eating, I snuck over the fence into Haggerty's pool and drank some water from a garden hose. I took a nap in the shade of my board. When I awoke, I threw up the sand crabs and paddled back out through the small cove waves and out into the big ocean.

From the horizon rose a fog wave, painting over the blue walls of the sky an omniscient, inscrutable gray. A weathered surfer reads the surf from the highway, from the bluff overlooking the cove, from the parking lot before exiting the surf truck, from the beach, from the water. The surfer reads the surf incessantly, studying the swell direction, size, intervals, watching the waves build, break, roll, and wash out through rips.

It is easy to sentimentalize surfing, to wax romantic about the ocean, to fantasize about oceanic feelings, but I was not a poet, nor a scientist, not a fisherman, nor a seascape painter. I was not an artist. I was just a surfer, another board on the water. I might have been like a sculptor, but the playful sport of surfing should not be taken too seriously. The dolphins don't take it seriously, and they are the best surfers in the world. Penina accused me of attempting to add meaning, of looking for something that is not there. "Kick out," I heard Henry Killknot saying. "The whole thing's closing out on you, a total wipeout," Henry had said. "Surfing is essentially useless. Yes, it might be meditative, and exercise is not useless, but a necessity, but you're trying to take surfing and make it into architecture, or worse, sculpture. Surfing is free of art, simple, not deceitful. It's our only true sport. Not man against man, and not man against nature, but the sport of blending purposefully with the salt and fish and porpoises and yes the very whales with the wild waves of Mother Earth." Penina had heard this last part more than once and the last time I had repeated it to her she had rolled her eyes so far up and away I thought she was fainting.

Killknot was at least right that surfing is more like

sculpture than architecture. Up on the beach, the surfers brag and succumb to fads, fall for music, dress to blend in with a crowd, buy a board that hangs from the rafters in the garage, never feeling the water. But in the water, the surfer is unable to fool the ocean. Killknot bemoaned the direction the sport was taking toward commercialization and competition, where a legendary surfer could be a teenager, but attempts to philosophize surfing at that age was advertising, and what have you got, anyway – nothing, Henry had said. In the end, the surf's down, water flat, tide in, trash in the waves, beach dirty, littered with garbage from weekend tourists, needles, used condoms, birds strangled in fishline, the blackball flag up, and you're sunburned and dry and back to pounding nails, digging ditches, laying pipe, spreading plaster, cutting glass, hanging cabinets, sanding blanks, or drinking beer, sniffing resins and glues, or getting stoned. Kick out, before you go over the falls. All this was Henry Killknot still ringing in my ears, but Henry was now gone. Henry had kicked out, pulled out when there was still plenty of wave.

"You think too much," Henry had said. "While most surfers spend their mornings surfing, afternoons getting stoned, and evenings getting laid, you're out paddling around the bay on some misbegotten Pilgrim's Progress. And when you come out of the water, you've got your head stuck in that notebook. Jump in, take

212

one, surf, but then get out, go to work, go to school. That's all there is to it, man. Don't give me all this crap about your oceanic feelings. The ocean doesn't feel anything. You're overwriting life now. You're turning the ocean into a turbid pool of purple prose." But it now appeared that Henry was the one who thought too much, or thought too ill, and I was the one who simply wanted to surf, and that was all I valued.

In the evening, the bay blistered with breezes popping into flickering shards of glass fracturing into white caps. In the morning, I awoke just before dawn, the water flat and glassy, the rolling swells thick and deep and long, the bay solid, a thick jell. I paddled toward the nearest break and began surfing at dawn.

It was too late for me to paddle back in, to rejoin the others, to adjust to Penina's needs and wants. I had passed that point every surfer knows and dreads. I fell, was falling, over the falls, into a mysterious dark wave. "Ah, hell," I can hear Henry saying, and probably he's right. Still, I bustled about the bay, feeling productive, catching waves. I basked in a sedulous secret. "What the hell does that mean?" Henry would have asked. The sea seethed and boiled, while Penina rolled her eyes into the back of her head.

I missed Henry, goofball that he was. Once, when the surf was flat, we went swinging in a park. Henry likened the swinging to surfing. It was silly, but Henry was fun when he wasn't stuck on his family problems, when he wasn't busy hating his father, hating the church and everything in it, hating Father Lynch. I once asked Henry to count the number of times he used the word hate in a day, then count the number of times he used the word love. Henry was a hater, and what he hated most was Henry. But he wasn't stupid and he wasn't a phony. He hated himself for being the hater he was.

Fogs formed as in a marshy swamp. At night a dark sea beast crawled beneath my surfboard. I heard sounds like a wild pig sucking her compost soup. I was juiced in it, soaked to the gills, a dripping thing myself, the bay a water pot. I paddled on, the sea beast emitting a dim glow from below, sounding deeper and deeper, sonorous burping bubbles rising. I drifted with the current and tide, pulled through furrows of swells, until I fell asleep, floating on the water wherever the currents and breezes and swells carried me.

In the morning I awoke with no idea where I was, where I had been, where I was going. I might have been a piece of driftwood, floating with the swells. I had broken off the mother tree in an evil storm. Henry groans and Penina shakes her head and Puck pounds on his workbench. But I jumped up, stretched, dove in for an awakening swim, diving in a short arch, coming up through the light water, blowing the night muck out my nose, clearing my head, shaking my short but wild mop of sea wrack hair, getting a new coat of salt that sealed my skin, and I paddled away in the direction of the swell looking for a beach with some waves.

I was a surfer. I was not born a surfer. I learned to surf, taught myself to surf, decided to surf, every day, every wave. Surfing is a virtue, each wave a sculptured grace, a gift.

From the bay I watched the local surfers cruise Highland Avenue down through the beach cities, radios on, checking out the surf, their vans gleaming slugs smoking like campfires.

I was a surfer. I grew bulbous calloused knots on the top of my feet and on my knees. I studied the light on the architecture of the waves, but an architecture that was pure sculpture. I was a student, away at sea, but close, in the bay, where Penina could find me. I was not confused. I knew what I wanted. I wanted to surf in the mornings, work in the afternoons, drink a few beers at the end of the day, and sleep with Penina through the night.

I surfed and slept, living on the cool blue bay. The sun's fan edged light sprayed over me. The sound I heard awakening was my own laughter. What a wastrel I was, adrift, my only purpose to surf, to float about in the bay, wordless as a fish. My brain picked up radio stations skipping across the water, and music filled my head. I caught a few waves and paddled about, talking to no one.

I touched dolphins and whales. Other things in the water jazzed by like shooting stars. I saw sea otters, jelly fish, floating debris. Other dark shapes drifted under my surfboard, silently slithering, or quickly darting shadows. California pelicans landed on the water near me. I was sitting on my board, legs dangling in the water, watching the Palos Verdes Peninsula, and thinking of paddling into the Redondo wharf for some fish scraps, when a pelican landed on the end of my board. Another sea lion surfaced near, looking like the same wet dog that had greeted me when I first paddled out to live on the water. In the evening, the night sky smeared like oil paint, thinly brushed clouds, the sky polished to a sheen like beeswax on smooth wood. I was on my back on my surfboard, looking up. I was thinking of the family home and of Penina again.

We had walked under palm trees, pepper trees, eucalyptus trees, in shadows and shade. We never closed our windows, and the climbing scarlet tomato red bougainvillea grew into the house. We felt the simple happiness that comes from the feel of walking with bare feet through patches of green grass up to views over brown dunes down to the blue water. But the sea is constantly at work on the land, while on land man is at work in the dunes, building, tearing down, and building again. Our simple Eden wasn't to last. It wasn't even ours. We were renters. And now, how to be, or how not to be, that was my question. I was still a young man, and still in that space of adjustment, as Sergeant Williams called it, between a war and home, between coming home and finding Penina. What was I doing out on the water, living on the bay, sleeping on my surfboard, eating like a fish crabs out of tide pools?

Surfing is dangerous. I comprehended the ocean without understanding it. Ominous ocean sounds continued to lick up into the bay breezes toward dusk. The sun fell, crashed, ripping red holes through a purple fabric, through garden clouds lingering, lofting like billowing curtains on the ceiling of my living room. I didn't have to talk to anyone. I was free of words, liberated from language. Waves like empty pages blew toward the beaches.

I awoke not knowing where I was. At night I drifted with the swells and currents and breezes and winds. The water on the surface is not the same as the winds aloft. The momentary confusion I felt at dawn invigorated me. The wind had turned around, or fell off, or turned off shore. Again I surfed all day long. I paddled in to Refugio. I could see Penina and Puck and some of the others, the same ones that had read Penina's letters aloud at the party, save Henry, of course, who had blown himself up, his hate igniting, his hair aflame, a pathetic Pentecost, abandoned by the tongues of his fathers. They were gathered in the courtyard outside Puck's shop, sitting around a roughly hewn oak table made from bridge planks, under a grape arbor lit by lanterns. I could smell Puck's pungent carob trees as the wind began to shift again, off shore. Puck had his arm around Penina.

I awoke to find myself ensconced in a thick milky fog, as thick as a bowl of oatmeal. I could not see the water. Everything had disappeared, no sounds, no sight but a thick light gray wetness, salty. In a wave, thought meets action so quickly there is no time for anxiety. Angst is a measure on land. The blank slate of the ocean slapped flatly under my board. I couldn't fall off. On the ocean, only the light and the sculpture of the waves bore significance.

I sat on my board deep in the bay, looking east toward shore and Los Angeles. I could see County Line to the north, Leo Carrillo Beach, the rippling canyons up above the beaches, Muscle Beach at Venice, the Hyperion sewage treatment plant at El Segundo. I followed Century past the hotels, or Imperial past the airport, all the way up to the Watts Towers. I saw Rancho Dominguez on the plateau up behind Manhattan. I watched the surfers going down to the beaches with their boards, carrying the boards against their hips, or balanced on their heads, until they reached knee deep water and dropped the surfboard with a flat splat and tossed the salty white foam over the waxed surface of the board. I watched them waiting for a lull in the rush of surf, push the board forward, slipping on, smoothly, prone, paddling head up through the waves and past the break, paddling out. The surfers burrowed into the waves for shade, for shelter, naked to the sculpture and the light. The ocean provides space, an expanse beyond the brain. The ocean rises and fills one's fancy with the frills of waves.

At dawn, the sun rising over the Los Angeles basin, always the same spreading light, the liquid pouring, and the golden particles bouncing like bees of pure energy, the palms lighting up green, I paddled back in to catch some waves. The light from the basin spilled against the waves, bouncing off the blue and white stuccoed sky walls beneath the red slate sun. I could hear Penina on her guitar, now singing the blues like a slow distant ransacking, like a train pulling out, going somewhere, the tracks leading up away from the jetty and away from the water. I had paddled out to live on my surfboard, to clear my thoughts, to calm my thoughts, to rid myself of unwanted thoughts, to escape my anxieties, and because the sounds of the water drowned out the sounds in my head. How long might I pretend to live on the water?

From the water I studied the Los Angeles basin. I looked

in garages and saw surfers reshaping and shortening their boards. They would not be able to live on the water as I did, on boards so short. They had realized they could ride a two-by-four as a surfboard if they could reach the proper momentum. I could see the empty lot where I had grown up, where my parents' house had sat, before the airport expansion had destroyed the neighborhood, and I remember the day my father asked me what I wanted to do with my life. He meant what I wanted to do for work, for a job.

He had awaited my answer, but I looked out at the ocean. Small clouds of white water broke over the jetty rocks. The swell was thick and the waves fat and the waves would not break outside the jetty but waited until they hit the rocks. The rocks came up to punch the swells in their guts, and the waves fell over onto the rocks, pouring through the rocks. No one was out. These were not waves a surfer could ride. My father waited for an answer. He waited a long time. He died waiting. And now here I was, living on the water, living on a 14' 7" dinged up and patched over surfboard. The board had just come in to Puck's shop a week or so prior. It was an original from the pioneering O'Sean's surfboard shop on Pacific Coast Highway in Hermosa Beach. Puck had asked me to peel it clean and reshape it into a smaller board. I said no to this one, no way.

"It's a classic. I'm going to live on this thing," I joked.

"Whatever," Puck said, "but we need some more short boards in the shop."

And what of the whale? Nothing. And of living on the water? A mere story, fiction, something to write about, a pursuit, surfing, like sailing, to stare off suicide, to stave off Henry's kind of wipeout. A sailor rarely thinks of suicide with his hand on the tiller. Nor does a surfer think of killing himself when he's taking off on a wave. He thinks of making it, of making the wave, of reaching the shoulder, of riding the wave to its natural conclusion. I don't want to write a big, significant book filled with battles or domestic scenes. Before the reader even gets to the first line, he has to read through an inside chop of quotes, like paddling out through the foamy white water of a beach break, the great open ocean looming. But what do I have to add ballast? So I went to live on the Bay, to have something to do, to occupy my time, like a writer. I would not think of committing suicide living on the water. And like a reader, a surfer, a sailor, I read the ocean.

I guess we might tell ourselves stories, our own stories, trippingly true, easy to falsify, even if we are the only ones who will ever hear them. But why should someone have to live with the story they've been handed down, knowing those stories too are readymade inventions? But it's not so easy to dismiss or retell how the story is handed down, how the story is told. A writer can make up a new story, but if he tells it in the same used way, he may not have much of a new story. I suppose if he could put together all the true parts of all these stories and leave out all the false parts, he might then have some idea of the truth of things. But no, we are always adding and subtracting, embellishing and erasing, sending our readers, who should be our friends, down dead ends, putting them off, setting them up, avoiding details, including irrelevancies, throwing everyone off track, doctoring up photos, putting on a prepared face, pretending loss, tossing some letters, saving others, one minute dressing to best the boulevard and the next minute trying to hide behind a telephone pole or scurry down a rabbit hole. We tell stories to avoid the truth of things, but in the end, the truth tricks us all. Nor could I hide on the water. I could not hide from Penina, from Puck, from Henry, or from myself.

I paddled back in and walked up to the shop.

"Where the hell have you been for the past three days," Puck Malone yelled. "I was worried sick about you, man. And we got orders here. Surf club down in Orange County wants nine new boards, man. Dig it," Malone said, throwing the order for the new boards across the counter at me.

"But what the hell, man. And you don't tell Penina where

you're going? Just because she's pissed doesn't mean she's not still worried about you, man. Where you been? This better be good."

"I told Penina where I was going."

"Yeah, yeah, going to live out on Santa Monica Bay, on a surfboard. What the hell kind of nonsense is that?"

"Where is Penina now?"

"She packed up and headed out, man, plenty pissed, too. She slept alone here one night, waiting for you, and the next day moved over to Angel's place in Gundo."

Puck and I got something to eat while I told him all about how I had lived on the water for three days, how I had paddled out to live on the water, leaving Penina stranded up on the beach. He didn't say anything. At one point he shook his head back and forth. When I had finished he said, "You're crazy, man. Know that? Lunatic. You expect me to believe you been out living on the water day and night for three days? No way, man, no way. What the fuck are you trying to prove, making that kind of shit up?"

"Believe what you want, Puck. What do you think, I dreamed it?"

"That's just your problem, Salty. Life is not some copout dream."

"That might be a perfect description, actually. But if life is a dream, whose dream is it?"

"Now what is that supposed to mean?"

"Who's dreaming it, you or me?"

"You know what you got with all this living on the water for three days and nights and all that crap? That's a case of what do you call it? That figure stuff you told me about? How you used it in Penina's letters and all. Figure language. No, figuring language."

"Figurative language."

"Yeah, that's what I said, figuring language, only there ain't no money in it, honey."

"There might be some money in it."

"How?"

"Suppose the story got out about how I spent three days and nights living on the Santa Monica Bay on a surfboard. That's the stuff legends are made of. Instead of giving me a bad time, you ought to be thinking of naming a surfboard after me. Kids all up and down the beach cities would be lining up to get a look at the legend and his surfboard. And putting in an order for one."

I could tell Puck was considering this.

"I don't know, man. Kids are getting into these short boards. But you might be on to something there. I'll think about it.

But it's not like you, selling out surfing like that. You're trying to throw me off what's important here. You leave that figuring language stuff alone. You want to know what figuring language is?"

"What?"

"I'm going to tell you right now what that figuring language is all about. Crazy talk, that's all that is, lunatic jive. Poetry. Let me tell you something about poetry, man. Poetry sucks. If you have something to say, say it, no ruffles and nothing to worry about, no confusion. No wonder Penina's worried blind about you, talking all that figuring language stuff."

"You once told me you could tread water for three days. What kind of figuring language was that?"

"I can tread water for three days. You can't tread water for three minutes without having to write some goddamn poem about it."

"Tell you what, Puck. I'm zonked from living on the water three days. Let's eat, and I'll turn in early and get some sleep, and come morning I'll get back to work."

"All right, man, all right," Puck said, shaking his head up and down. "That's the first sane thing you've said since you came out of the water. And if there's any more figuring language necessary, let me do it. You're no good with numbers to begin

225

with. You get some sleep, and in the morning, climb back on board, Salty, come on in, for real, buddy. And take a shower, man. I'm not just figuring language when I say you smell like a really bad oyster."

I went back to my room and wrote Penina another letter before crashing and sleeping soundly through the night.

Dear Penina:

I'm back from my ocean sojourn, three nights living out in the bay. It wasn't so hard living on the water. I surfed all day and paddled back out at night. At first, I thought I might be able to eat out of the coves at Palos Verdes, on abalone or sand crabs, but it's not possible from the water. I paddled up to the fishing barge anchored off Redondo. Captain Elias took me aboard and fed me fish and beer. He offered me a place to sleep aboard the barge. I wanted to sleep on the ocean on my surfboard, but of course that was crazy talk. But I did stay one entire night on the water. I felt the predawn fizz of the water filling with anticipation of the coming of the sun, and I floated, fortuitously, deracinated and perhaps deranged, into the barge. Elias was pulling up some nets that had been out all night, and putting a spotlight on me, scrambled down the barge ladder to the water to help me. I lived on the ocean for three nights, two on the barge, paddling back in each morning to surf all day. I paddled back out to the barge in the evening.

Captain Elias told some tall tales. He loaned me some clothes, a heavy shirt and some baggy pants to put on, and we stayed up late, gam-swapping stories.

"So, what's your tale?" he asked me, taking a long swig from a silver hip flask engraved with a catboat. I didn't get his meaning.

"Your tale is your obsession, your destiny, your fate. Is your tale a wild woman, bad thoughts, or a risky activity?" he asked. "A hatred or a fear, a love or a desire? A business, a church, a government?"

"Are those my only choices?"

Elias served in the Navy in the Great War, and again in the Pacific in the next war, but he sat the next one out, he said, wanted nothing more to do with war, but shipped out with the Merchant Marine, and finally took the job as captain of the fishing barge. He was content to live on the ocean, an exile from the mainland, from the land of man. He's an old man now, face of weathered, cracked bladderwrack, wild, white hairs sprouting from his ears and nose and above his black eyes and curling out the back of his cap down to his shoulders. He's the only one living full-time on the barge. He lives on the water.

"Of all the men I've ever asked that question to, the answer always seems to come down to one of three tales: a woman, a mental condition, or work."

"Could the answer not be all three, at once?"

"Nah. You water the answer down. Focus, my boy. There's only ever one tale for each of us. What is yours? A partner you can't seem to live in peace with, bad thoughts you're unable to escape from, or a job you seem ill-suited to but are afraid to abandon or to lose?"

"I don't know that I have any bad thoughts, at least not while surfing."

Captain Elias built a bonfire in a rusted steel drum on the deck of the barge. There were three others on board for the night, fishing off the sides of the barge, using sardines to catch flounder. In the distance we could see the lights of the South Bay beach cities. The Captain asked me about my war. I told him a story about a refugee I had helped.

Penina, do you remember the little black and white photo of you and me on the beach in front of a wave at El Porto, which I kept in my wallet throughout the war?

I told Captain Elias about a refugee boat that had capsized offshore. The boat had been too full, refugees piled on top of one another, all trying to escape the war. The boat was a simple fishing boat, not designed to carry so many people across rough waters. In the morning, we started to pick up refugees who had made it to shore. I helped one skinny, teenaged boy come out of the water. We had set up a water purification unit up from the beach, and a small, temporary shelter, a tent with some cots. I got the boy something to drink and eat. A Red Cross nurse took a look at him and said he'd be okay. He spoke a little English. He said his name was Jack, a name he had used before, no doubt, when having to work with us. He explained he had been with a friend. They had walked down from the north, sleeping in the day and walking at night. They'd been on the run for three days when they got to the village with the boat leaving, and they hopped on board at the last minute.

We had other work to do in the area, and I lost track of Jack. Toward evening, a couple of days later, he walked back into our camp. I got him food and spent some time talking to him. I showed Jack the picture in my wallet. Now I had to explain to Captain Elias who you are, Penina, as I explained to him that I pointed to you in the picture, trying to explain who you were to Jack. I showed Jack the beach in the photo, El Porto, and tried to explain where I had come from, the beach, and how much I loved the water, the ocean, waves and the surf. I told Elias that Jack's response was to point to the wave in the photo and tell me he had found his friend's bloated body washed up on the beach that morning. He said he didn't like waves, and he didn't like the beach or the water, and he wanted to go back to his farm.

Jack took off, and I was alone on the beach holding my snapshot of a boy I no longer was and his girl I might no longer know or recognize. The picture was fading, worn, cracked. The wave looked like an old doily fragment, the threads unraveling. There was a crack across my forehead that looked like a scar. I had scaly eyes. I touched your face with my fingers, touched your hair. It was now late evening, and the guys were starting to turn in. I walked down the beach to the water. It was a very quiet night. The water was flat, small ripples breaking at the edge of the beach, receding quickly. A lustrous, vulnerable moon, a metal-flaked moon, turned the water silver.

Penina, I held the picture of you and me and the wave on the beach at El Porto and tossed it into the water. It floated for a few seconds until a tiny ripple broke over it. But tonight I feel differently. I'd like to have that photo back. What do the waves want? The saucy waves want to wrap around your thighs, but the foam says shush. You are a being silent. When I grow old and numb from the water, I'll skiff a lid of paper over my ocean, and the quiet rest of the beach will feel good. The moon's echo falls across the sand, spreads though the cove where the grasses grow all the way down to the water, to a shore pound wave that keeps collapsing into itself, the tide too high. Above us, the palm fronds trill in an onshore breeze. We've lived here since birth, up from the beach, the waves at night coming closer and closer. We can't leave the ocean. The waves still crash. We hear the water recede and rise, recede and rise. A spray of salty kisses falls on us. Every glance you give is a wave. Each glance in its turn recedes. Yet the water still rises. We walk through wickets of waves, children playing on the beach at El Porto. But tonight the waves are all closed, the water is still, and I call your name, and the warm waves of your hair curl like cattails brushing my cheeks, and I awake, and there you are, sleeping next to me, sleeping in the distant silence of the dunes up from the beach, up above the water, and even the ocean is for once at rest, sleeping.

Only Captain Elias is still awake, walking his bridge, on the lookout for lost at sea surfers and other drowning water people.

Love, Sal

PS: Puck's a bit miffed that I took off without telling him where I was going, so I've got to pay some dues and work hard in the shop for a few days. But let's do something tomorrow evening after work. Maybe we'll go down to the La Mar and catch a flick.

~ ~ ~

How to Surf

I had just come out of the water and was sitting on my surfboard above the high tide line where the sand was dry and the morning sun felt warm on my back. The tide was out, the waves flat, and the break was a long way off, maybe a hundred yards or more, and the low walls of white foam rolling over the flat, shallow water nearer shore created a gentle surf condition ideal for someone wanting to learn how to surf. The surf was quiet, no hollow booms of bull waves that sometimes struck El Porto mornings. It was still morning yet, but with the sun on my back, my skin was already drying, little salt-crumb flakes drying on the hairs on my shoulders and arms and the back of my hands. A few late morning sunbathers dotted the beach, their bright blue or green or orange umbrellas sticking up out of the sand over rumpled, colorful beach towels. Two children were building a sand castle in the wet sand down closer to the water. They were hard at work with red and white plastic buckets and toy shovels. One of them, a boy, was digging a hole in their sand castle courtyard, digging down to the water, pulling up sand crabs, while the other, a girl, was forming the wet sand into a rampart to protect the castle against an incoming tide. Two young women had set up an umbrella and towels up the beach and just off to my side, also above the tide line, and were sitting in beach chairs. One was reading a book, the other a magazine. They had on floppy sun hats and wore sunglasses and were listening to what sounded like top 40 songs on a transistor radio. They had brought an olive drab canvas raft down with them that leaned against a bright red cooler. Behind them, farther up the beach, a bright yellow, county lifeguard truck dropped off one of the lifeguards to open the 42nd Street tower.

The lifeguard unlocked the tower door, went inside, and lifted open the wood windows, leaning out to latch them to the cantilevered roof. He was open for business. He then came down near where I was sitting and set up a no surfboard zone with flagpoles stuck in the sand at the top of the tide berm. The lifeguard recognized me and waved and yelled my name. It was Jack Fisher, one of the high school water polo champs out of El Segundo. Jack shook his head slowly back and forth and pointed at me with his orange lifeguard can, which I took for a recognition gesture for my recent deep-water, Santa Monica Bay feat. I watched him stick his buoy-can in the sand at the bottom of the tower and climb slowly up the ramp to his beach chair where he would sit out the long day. He would not get much business today in the easy surf. I did not envy the lifeguards, confined in their small, hot towers for purgatorial, pepper-hot days without much to do but listen to the radio. Their rules prohibited reading. They were to keep their eyes on the water, visors and sunglasses necessary to protect against water-glare scald. They could sit on the deck outside the tower, and often did, but by late spring their skin would have already turned a burnt red-sienna, and they had to rub gobs of gooey lotions into their skin. Jack Fisher had his nose and cheeks smothered with a bright white zinc oxide. He was wearing the bright red swim trunks of the lifeguard.

I glanced around to look at the young women again, who I assumed were the mothers of the children working on the sand castle, and one of them caught my eye looking at her and gave me a small, tentative wave, as if she was not sure of something. She got up and started walking toward me.

"Are you Salty?" she asked.

"Yes," I said, standing up.

"I thought I recognized you. I'm Laura, Suzie Shea's older sister."

"Oh, yeah, of course, and I recognize you now. How are you?"

"I'm fine, thanks. You got home from the Army."

"Yes."

"What are you doing now that you're back?"

"Surfing, mostly," I laughed, "and shaping boards. How's Suzie doing? I've not seen her."

"I saw Tom's parents. They said you had stopped by to say hello."

"Yes, and they mentioned Suzie, but it didn't sound like they see her much anymore. How is she?"

"She doesn't like going over there anymore. She's engaged again."

"Well, good for her. Say hi for me, and give her my congratulations. Anyone I might know?"

"I doubt it. Someone she met where she works. His name is Matt Yalper, big executive in some downtown insurance firm."

"Downtown Los Angeles?"

"Yes, big time."

"Wow. Well, no, I don't know him."

"Well, anyway, she seems happy with him. Though she still thinks of Tom often.

"Yes. It was so sad seeing his parents, so lost in their sadness."

"You're lucky you missed the funeral."

"Yeah, so I heard."

I didn't know Laura well. She and Suzie and Tom had all

grown up and gone to school in El Segundo. Tom had been a good surfing buddy of mine, but girlfriends regularly pulled surfers out of the water and away from the beach. Laura looked over at the children building the sand castle, fixing her hair behind her ears with her fingers. She was wearing a bright yellow sun hat but had taken off her sunglasses to talk to me. Her long, wavy hair was dark and her skin nut brown like a dark olive and oiled with suntan lotion. She wore a light, open blouse over a modest, two-piece suit, the blouse hanging down to her thighs, the same, practical outfit a generation of beach women had grown up wearing. She looked at the water, at the children, and back at me. She seemed to be waiting for me to say something more.

"And the sand castle builders, you belong to them?" I said.

"Yes. That's my son, Jonah, and my daughter, Joy."

"How old are they?"

"Jonah is six, and Joy is four."

She called to the kids and they came running over to us. Joy wrapped her arms around her mom's legs, and Jonah stood by, looking with interest at my surfboard. Laura introduced her kids to me.

"This is Salty. He knows Suzie. And he knew Suzie's boyfriend Tom. Salty got back from the Army not too long ago."

"Are you a surfer?" Jonah asked.

"Yeah. Are you a surfer?"

"I don't know how to surf," Jonah said.

"I see you have a surf mat up on the beach. Do you ride the surf mat?"

"Sometimes, if my mom takes us out, but she almost never does."

"You want to go a little ways out on my surfboard?"

"I don't know how."

"I'll go with you."

"Yes, yes," Jonah said, shaking his head up and down and looking to his mom for approval.

"Oh, I don't know," Laura said.

"Please, Mom, please."

"Not too far out," Laura said.

"We'll just be right here, in the soup close in," I said.

"Okay. We'll be watching you. Hold on tight. Not too far out," she said, looking at me.

The first time I took a surfboard into the water, I was in a Junior Lifeguard program in Manhattan Beach. We paddled out through the surf and around a buoy and rode the white water prone on our boards into shore. We were told not to stand, even if we thought we already knew how. Still, at the end of the exercise, a number of empty boards were washed up on the beach, their riders caught in the surf, dogpaddling through the soup. There is no easy way to learn to surf, no way to learn to catch and ride waves that does not include a few wipeouts.

I walked with Jonah down to the water's edge and put the board down and showed him how to rub some wet sand into the wax to rough it up a bit so he wouldn't slip off the board. Then I pushed the board forward into about a foot or two of water. I told Jonah to walk next to me, next to the board, and not get behind the board.

"Okay, Jonah. Let's just stand here next to the board and let a few waves wash through."

We were standing in shallow water, and the white water from the waves breaking farther out reached us in small, one-foot tall walls of weak, slushy foam. I looked around and saw Laura holding Joy's hand, standing in the wet sand at the water line. Jonah looked around and waved vigorously to his mom and sister, and they both waved back.

"You stand in front of me, Jonah, and I'll be right behind you. Put your arm across the board, like this, and hold on to the other side with your hand, like this. Hold the rail. This edge of the board all around is called the rail. Keep most of the board behind you. Keep the nose pointed forward, pointed to the waves. When the next wave comes, we'll hold the nose of the board up over the white water, and the white water will wash under the board."

We stood in the shallow water next to the surfboard. Jonah looked back at me, and the expression on his face suggested he was absorbing the cardinal surfer epiphany that the surf looks different from the water than it does from shore, always bigger.

"Do you ride a skateboard?" I asked Jonah.

"I have one. But I don't ride it much. My mom won't let me go up the hill."

"Doesn't matter. Learning to ride waves is not like learning to ride a skateboard," I said. "Sidewalks don't move under the rider on a skateboard. When you surf, you have to learn to read the water and the waves, and keep watch out for other surfers and their surfboards. And sometimes you might see other hazards in the water. And some beaches have special hazards like the pipes at El Segundo."

The waves were breaking far apart, at long intervals. The water seemed lazy, sleepy. Some of the small walls of white water were fizzling out before they reached us. I walked Jonah farther out into the water, and a wave of white water came rushing toward us.

"Here comes the wave. Lift up the nose." The curling white water soup washed under our surfboard.

"What's a hazard?" Jonah asked.

"A hazard is something in the water, or under the water, like rocks or pipes or sandbars or seaweed. Or a loose surfboard washing in to shore without a surfer."

"What about fish?"

"Yeah, but we don't have too many fish in the beach break here at El Porto."

Jonah still had the skinny arms and legs of a little boy. Most surfers I knew were in good, balanced shape, physically, but I had lately been hearing more rumors of surfers taking to the waves drunk or stoned. But surfing is dangerous, and the ocean, like most of nature, suffers no hallucinations. Yet propelled by the force of hundreds of miles of wind and water currents, swells can go crazy when they finally reach a beach. Nothing is as breakneck drunk and unpredictable as the surf. Most surfing around beaches like El Porto is done in the cool, early morning hours, when the waves are glassy and the breeze is offshore, holding the wave's face open. By afternoon, at a beach break like El Porto, the wind turns around and starts to blow in off the ocean, onshore, pushing the waves over, creating choppy conditions, and the waves lose their glass, and the face of the wave closes quickly. But in late summer, El Porto often enjoys a late afternoon or early evening glass off, when the wind falls silent and the water comes in smooth and glassy like a morning break. The sandy bottom is brushed smooth, and in low tides the waves break in shallow water far from shore.

"We'll stand here awhile holding on to the board and watch the waves coming in, and when the soup gets close, we'll keep lifting the nose up over the surf. That way we'll get used to the water and we'll know how the waves are coming in, how fast and how hard and how often."

Jonah was too small to handle a board on his own, but what he was getting now was the sense of being in the water with a surfboard, a sense of the movement of the waves and the buoyancy of the board on the water. The old surfboards were made from redwood or balsawood, but the newer surfboards were made from foam blanks skinned with fiberglass and resin. A supportive, wood strip strengthening the foam like a truss rod ran the length of the board.

"See the wood strip?" I asked Jonah, rubbing my fingers down the center of the board. "That's called the stringer. You should get to know the names of things. The fin is called a skeg. The skeg is attached to the bottom tail of the board. The fin stabilizes the board and helps you turn the board. The skeg is like the rudder of a boat."

The boards Puck and Henry and I had learned to ride when we were young were made from foam blanks resined with fiberglass, with a single, wood stringer and a large, single fin setup. In Malone's shop, we now worked on a mix of board styles. I was still interested in longboards, and Puck was too, but he saw that the shorter boards, introducing multiple-fin setups, adding corner skegs to a smaller center skeg, were becoming popular. The short boards were more than a fad, and the young surfers grabbing them up seemed more interested in the trappings and paraphernalia of popular surf culture than in waves and the ocean. A young kid might come into the shop with his father, and his father would put down as much money for wet suit and tee shirts and shorts and trunks and sandals and posters as he did for the surfboard. And the shorter boards were ridden with a different surfing style. The tone of surfing seemed to be changing. Puck and I would soon be old-timers.

The surfboard Jonah and I were in the water with was just over ten feet long and two feet wide in the middle. It was big and buoyant and stable. We held the board perpendicular to the oncoming waves. I was now standing in water up to my knees. The board rose easily over the incoming foam, but Jonah, much shorter than me, was now jumping up to keep the soup from splashing his face. It was time to get on the board.

"Okay, Jonah, now let's get on the board. I'm going to help you slide onto the board. Hold the rails with both hands."

I knew Jonah was nervous now. Smooth surfing, the surfer blending with the wave's movement, comes from relaxed muscle control, from being relaxed in the water.

"Okay, Jonah, let's wait some more. We don't have to rush. I'm just going to stand here next to you and hold the board with you on it, and we'll just stay here and let some more waves wash under us."

I pushed the surfboard forward while sliding onto it into a prone position, covering Jonah, and paddled slowly.

"Can you feel how we're balanced?"

"Yes."

"Let's paddle forward, and keep the nose of the board up, and when the next wave comes, we'll lean back so the nose comes up over the white water. I'll hold on to you. You keep your hands on the rail."

Our tail was down and we were trim in the water, and I paddled forward with cupped hands. The first wave that hit us lifted us up and rolled under us.

"Did you feel that, Jonah, the wave rolling under us?"

"Yes."

"That's what you want, the wave to roll under you like that. Let's keep paddling out slowly."

We paddled out, letting the waves roll under the board, and we soon reached the break, where the waves were turning slowly over into whitewater, or soup, the stuff we'd been letting slip under our board, leaning back and raising our heads. Jonah seemed comfortable on the board, leaning back, holding the rails and pushing up onto his extended arms and raising his head above the foam as the waves washed through.

I was watching and judging the incoming swells, the breaking waves, for a path to paddle through the break to the outside. There were no other surfers near us in the water, so I did not have any signals of outside waves that might be coming, and I couldn't judge from some surfer's behavior what the water conditions might be farther out. Watching other surfers usually will give clues to the surfer not as far out into the surf yet. I looked back to make sure we were still outside the no surf zone the lifeguard Jack Fisher had just set up with the red flags on the beach.

Surfing is a difficult sport that includes nature as part of the equipment. The flat gridiron of a football field does not suddenly rise to a ten percent slope and just as quickly fall. Puck had mentioned a surfing competition to take place down in

Huntington Beach. The organizers had invited him to participate as one of the judges. Of course, they had also asked him to donate a board and some tee shirts for prizes.

"Do the judges judge from the water?" I had asked Puck.

"Very funny," Puck said.

"They ought to at least set up the judging stand up on the pier, out over the waves," I said.

Puck saw surfing competition as a business opportunity, but I was not interested in competing with other surfers.

El Porto is not a big wave break, and the water there is mostly forgiving, but any size wave can break in surprise. The waves Jonah and I were paddling through were very small and slow, and the wave faces were not holding up long. The waves were breaking and coming over all at once, small but long walls. There was not much of a shoulder at either end of the wave. This surf posed little danger. When a skateboarder comes up off the asphalt pavement, bloody strawberry skin burns like peeling paint blistering his legs and arms, he wishes he had had the water landing of the surfer. Still, waves don't stand still like a concrete sidewalk, and I knew Laura, back at the water's edge, was probably full of anxiety.

I let several waves wash under the board, and Jonah was

having a good time now, and I could sense he had shed some of his nervousness, so in the next lull we swung the board around so that the nose was now pointed toward shore.

"Mom," Jonah yelled, waving, suddenly surprised at the view of the beach from the water, "look at me."

"I don't think she can hear you this far out, Jonah," I said, but Laura waved and put her hands over her face and watched us.

A swell floated toward us. I back paddled and side kicked to improve our position, Jonah beneath me, and paddled harder to gain some momentum. The swell reached us, lifted the board up and out of the water, and we felt lighter as we suddenly rushed forward. I did not try to angle but rode the wave straight, keeping the board's nose up and out of the white water as the wave crashed and we flew across the flat water rushing up into the wave. Jonah let out a yell, the sound of a stoked surfer. In the wave, Jonah was now a surfer, just as much a surfer as Henry, Humulus, Crux, Malone, me, or Tom Chippy had ever been.

We rode the wave of bubble water slush until the bottom of the board started to skid on the sand and I felt the skeg digging in, dragging. I slid off the board and let go, and Jonah and the board drifted forward, sliding to one side as the wave, now spent, stopped and receded, leaving Jonah high and dry. His mom and his sister came running.

"I want to go again," Jonah said. "Can you take me out again, Salty?"

Jonah and I paddled out again, a little farther this time, but still in the white water zone. We turned around and caught another little wave of slushy soup and rode it to shore.

"I want to stand up, Salty," Jonah said.

"Standing up takes time, Jonah. You need to be a good swimmer. If you fall, you need to be able to swim back in to shore. Can you swim?"

"A little."

"Let's go in and get the surf mat, and we'll paddle way out and catch a wave breaking."

We got out of the water and carried the board together, Jonah carrying the nose, up to the towels and umbrellas.

"Wow, isn't this exciting, Jonah?" Laura said.

"Yeah, mom. I guess I'm a surfer."

"I guess you are a surfer," Laura said, looking at me. "Is it good being a surfer, Sal?"

"I think so, Laura. Yeah, surfing is good."

I put the board down and asked Laura if Jonah and I could take the surf mat out. She hesitated, but quickly gave in to Jonah. I wondered a moment about Jonah's father, but didn't ask. We took the mat down to the water and paddled out to the break, turned, and caught a two foot wave, rising to the top and springing forward in a grand fall, Jonah screaming with delight, and rode the white water all the way to shore. We paddled out again and again. I taught Jonah to read the swells, and let him pick one. We began to drift southward some, and I wasn't watching the shore, and the next time I looked, Laura was at the water's edge waving us in. We caught one last wave and rode it to shore on the surf mat.

"How about you, Laura?" I said. "Want to go out on the mat with me?"

Laura gave me another questioning look. "Maybe some other time," she said, smiling, and we walked back up to the towels and umbrellas.

Laura's friend was another young woman, Lily Barth, but I did not know her. Laura introduced us, the kids ran back down to their sand castle, and I said goodbye to Laura and Lily, but Laura walked up the beach a short distance with me.

"Thank you for taking Jonah out. He was so excited."

"Oh, yeah. No problem. He seems like a good kid. Great fun, getting into the water."

"How's Penina?" Laura asked. We had stopped in the middle of the beach. "I have not seen her lately."

"Yeah, she's good, busy working and trying to finish school. Doesn't get down to the water much these days."

"I heard about Henry Killknot," Laura said. "He was a good friend of yours, wasn't he?"

"Yes, Henry. Henry wiped out."

"I'm sorry," Laura said.

"Yeah, well, not everyone who paddles out makes it back in, I guess. Something like that."

We looked back toward the water and Laura's children playing in their sand castle. Lily Barth was rubbing suntan lotion over her shoulders and arms.

"Goodbye, Sal. Welcome home. And thanks again for taking Jonah out into the water."

"Sure, and don't forget to say hi to Suzie for me."

"I will, for sure," Laura said, but she made no move to turn away. Once again, she stared at me quietly, as if waiting for me to say something more. We stood quietly like that for a few moments, and she did something that surprised me. She took a step toward me, grabbed my arms with her hands, and leaned in and kissed me on my left cheek. She let go, looking up into my eyes, and she spun around in the sand, and ran back toward the water, past the beach towels and umbrella, down to the sand castle and her children, where she turned around and saw me still watching her. She waved happily to me, and Jonah waved too.

The beginning surfer should not expect too much the first time out, but should be satisfied to turn the board around and ride the whitewater to shore in the prone position, holding the rails at ten and two o'clock, just above the head, weight back on the board to keep the nose up. Of the various forms of wipeout, to pearl, or pearling, is one of the most common to beginners. Pearling occurs when too much weight is shifted toward the nose of the board, causing it to dive into the water. When the nose of the board cuts into the water steeply, sharply, with speed, the result is a braking and reversing action of the board, and the surfer slips forward, over the handle bars, to use a bicycle analogy, landing in the water ahead of the board, the wave now catching the loose board akimbo and thrusting it forward, probably into the surfer, a perilous predicament, particularly if the board whips around sideways and parallel to the wave, the surfer catching the board broadside.

But if the white water is caught successfully, and the nose of the surfboard does not pearl, the surfer is now rushing to shore, torso and front half of the board ahead of the white water, the surfer's legs hidden in the soup. The new surfer is now stoked, and rides toward shore, all the way in, the wave rushing on either side, the flat water ahead rushing beneath the board. Riding prone for some distance gives the new surfer a feel for how the surfboard behaves in a wave.

One of the worst mistakes a new surfer can make is paddling successfully out into the break, past the white water and out past the breaking waves, without yet having developed enough skill to navigate the waves back to shore. This is a dangerous situation because once out past the break the surfer may be unable to either catch a wave or to paddle through the surf back toward shore. The surfer could get caught inside the breaking waves, and a wave could come crushing down on his back, or roll his board up into the wave face and hurl surfer and board forward. A new surfer out in the break is a menace to other surfers, has no self-reliance, and is a potential loose board. It sometimes seems easy to get out past the break, slipping easily out in a lull between wave sets, but that easiness can be a trap. When swells rise and reach the shallow areas of a surf spot, surfers scramble for position, choosing waves to catch, moving out, turning, glancing back over the shoulder, judging the water, feeling the speed and lift quicken. There is an existential point in any attempt to catch a wave that every surfer knows, even if things don't work out and the effort ends in a wipeout, a single split second in a long succession of blinking moments that quicken toward the break and the falling in to the wave. It's the point of catching the wave. It almost doesn't matter what comes next. The moment and movement meet and the surfer becomes one with the wave and must act. There's no escape, no pulling out, no turning back, no exit. No matter what else might happen now, the surfer is going forward with the wave. The surfer is always at one with the wave. Waves do peter out. No wave lasts forever. But the beginning surfer who wipes out, loses the board, and is caught under the churning wave may regret how easy it seemed to paddle out into the waves.

Beginning surfers should avoid crowded surfing conditions. It's better to surf a lesser wave in uncrowded conditions than paddle out into fine surf littered with boards. Most surfers in conversation bemoan crowds, hoard and protect their discovered secret spots, might try to intimidate outsiders at their local beach turf, but the average surfer will, paradoxically, school like a bird squatting on the water, bobbing up and down on the swells lazily, feigning disinterest, and some will sit that way for hours without ever catching a wave. It often seems that some surfers might not know how to get back in. Some surfers might not want to come back in. Lost, alone, and stranded in the surf, beyond the surf, surfers sometimes disappear, swallowed up by the ocean, enveloped in fogs, pulled under into seaweeds, run over by ships, eaten by fish, buried beneath waves.

I did not know if Jonah would become a surfer, if he'd

have the chance, if he'd get down to the water often enough, or if he'd be distracted by school, organized sports, work, cars, girls. A surfer's mind must be uncluttered, distilled, thoughts slowed to a drip, then off, then surf.

A couple of boards I had finished shaping were still sitting on drums and I needed to get back to work and get the boards glassed. Malone was concerned that we were falling behind on orders. I had been away living on the bay for three days, and when I got back, Puck and I had then taken a few days away from the shop to rebuild the front of Penina's apartment. We installed a new door and window and cleaned up the mess on the deck. Penina's harpoon had broken loose. We painted the wall above the deck and rehung the weathered log roller. Puck had found a couple of Penina's letters in the mess on the deck and handed them to her without comment. She took them inside, but I didn't see what she did with them. Across the alley, a couple of laborers had started cleaning out the shell of Henry's flash scorched apartment. Puck and I had walked over to take a look around inside. The blast had blown the roof upward, blown the windows and doors out, the roof dropping back down, and the apartment now sat awkwardly listing. An inside wall had fallen into the garage and smashed Henry's sports car. Puck went into the garage and salvaged one of the badges from the sports car, which had turned from a candy apple red to a streaked burnt sienna, and when we got back to Penina's, Puck nailed the badge over Penina's door.

And there was something else Puck had saved from Henry's place.

"Check this out," Puck had said, calling me over to a shelf built into the wall in Henry's place below a window that faced the Strand and the water.

Below the shelf, on the floor, lay a small statue, half buried in ash. I knelt down on one knee to pick it up. It was a cast bronze replication of Michelangelo's "Pieta," Mary holding her adult child across her knees. On the shelf was wedged a wood and glass frame, the glass cracked and shattered. Puck was trying to pull the box out from the shelf, and as he did, the remaining glass broke lose from the frame and fell to the floor. It was a shadow box.

"What the hell," Puck said. "It's a pair of panties," and he pulled from the box a bikini style, thin, silk panty, powder blue with tiny, white laced flowers around the fringe.

"They're Penina's," I said.

"How the hell you know that?"

"I bought them for her on my first leave. The squad had gone back up to the island for a weekend away from the war. I wrapped them around a letter and stuffed them into the envelope and mailed them to her."

"Jesus," Puck said.

"Yeah," I said.

"What should I do with them?" Puck asked.

"Give Penina her two letters back, but toss the panties. I think we should work on keeping things real."

"Amen to that, man."

We had walked back across the alley to Penina's, and on the way, Puck had tossed the panties into the dumpster the laborers were using to empty out Henry's apartment, and one of the laborers unceremoniously buried them under a shovelful of broken sheetrock, dust, and nails.

"When are you going to get those two boards still on the barrels glassed?" Puck asked. "We have to get those orders out, man, make room to start some new work."

It was early afternoon of the day I had talked to Laura on the beach. Puck and I were working on the week's schedule. Puck wanted me to drive the truck down to Redondo Beach with him. Some old guy was getting rid of some used, dinged up longboards Malone thought we could reshape into shorter boards. I told him we should keep them for rentals. His face lit up.

"Rentals, good idea. Surf mats, boards, skates. Maybe we should start selling food, snacks and pop and stuff, burgers and fries to go."

The shop was fast becoming unfiltered, cluttered.

"And lessons," I said. "We should start thinking about setting up a surf camp to give surfing lessons to kids."

"There you go, Salty. We're going to make a businessman out of you yet. Great idea. But why stop with kids? You think there might be a market for adults who want to learn how to surf?"

"I don't know. Let's start with the kids and see how it goes."

"I'm on board with the surf school idea," Puck said, smiling at his pun. "We'll need some teachers. We can recruit Lucas and that nut John Humulus."

"I don't know about Hops. You can't have surf teachers paddling out drunk with a bunch of kids in tow."

"Good point. We should get Penina to go in on this. She can handle the administrative stuff and maintain discipline in the school. Huh? And recruit some girls. We need to get more girls in the water. There's no reason girls can't surf. Untapped market there, surfboards for girls, shirts, sandals, surf jewelry, hats, dress tee shirts."

I worked through the afternoon glassing the two boards

that had been sitting on barrels for a few days. I cleaned up the workshop, swept up and took out the trash, and organized the tools. Puck had worked in the showroom all afternoon. Around five, he came back into my workroom to tell me he had just sold two boards to a couple of guys who had driven down from Malibu to check out the shop. Puck opened the icebox and pulled out a couple of beers to celebrate the sale.

We relaxed with a game of baseball darts while we drank the beers. In baseball darts, you aim at the 1 triangle in the first inning, the 2 in the second inning, and so on. I was the Dodgers and Puck was the Giants. Throwers have three darts per half inning, three chances to score. We counted darts in the triangle inning as one run, the double box as two runs, the triple box as three runs, and the bullseye was a grand slam. Puck won, 13 to 11, a close game.

We worked for another hour or so, and Puck went out to get us some fresh food. We ate on the counter in the showroom. A couple of kids came in, looked through all the boards, and bought a couple of "Puck's Surfboards" decals.

"I'm going up," I said. "I might want to do some writing before I come back down. I might have to get some sleep before coming back down to work. I'll be down later, and I'll work into the night."

"All right, man. Good day. Good work. I'm going to keep the shop open awhile longer, pencil out some of these new ideas. Puck's School of Surf! Ha! Love it! We'll offer degrees in surfing, credentials, designations. Brilliant, man."

I left Puck enthusiastically updating his business plan. I went up to my room thinking I might get some writing done but ended up falling asleep. When I awoke it was dark, and I went back down to the shop and worked into the night. It was after midnight when I got back up to my room. I had not seen nor heard from Penina. Since Puck and I had finished repairing her place, and she was now sleeping alone, back in her own bed, I saw her at irregular times. I sat down at my writing table and wrote another letter to Penina. Moonlight spread across my writing desk like a tablecloth, and the moon spread over the water in the distance, the waves flickering in the moonlight like fish scales.

Dear Penina:

I left you a note last night. I hope you got it. I said I would be home late. But now you are on your own again. We are on our own. And I can sleep right side up, my head in the moonlight, though I'd rather sleep head to toe with you than alone solo on my little pillow. My note said that Malone and I went down to Hermosa to watch the new surf film, "Wipeout Outre." Most of the film was devoted to wipeouts. Why do some guys wipeout? Some of these guys seemed to be asking for a wipeout, paddling into impossible waves, taking off too late, showing off for the camera, I guess. But the camera rarely follows them caught inside the break and does not capture them getting hit in the head with their board or watch them bleeding from a skeg wound. The surf film camera is a fickle device. Anyway, I taped the note to your icebox door, the fridge, frigid air. Funny we still call it an icebox. And yours is certainly small enough to qualify as an icebox, even if it is plugged in. Penina's icebox. Anyway, I walked down to your place after the film, and I didn't see the note, but I didn't see you either. And where are you tonight? Probably sleeping. I slept earlier, woke up, and worked on boards past midnight. Puck was in the film briefly as a truck full of boards cruised past his shop. Free advertising, he said. All he thinks about is business these days. One of these days, I'll throw a dart right at today and twang a bullseye. Pluck the ripe plumb, baby. Deplume the moments of your life, one piquant plume per moment. Can a wipeout be an epiphany? But I'm not sure I put much stock in epiphanies, the kick in the eye, the holy wake up call, the rude reminder, the spritz up our nose that blinds us eyes watering with grasping, gasping self-knowledge and awareness. Om mani padme hum. Oh, the kick in the ass. Eek, the epiphanic star whose light knocks us off our donkey. Nah, all the epiphanies I've ever had soon fizzled. But maybe I've just never gotten past the Om.

I saw Laura Shea this morning down at the beach. I took one of her kids out on my board, and we rode some white water waves. Great fun. Laura looked a little worried at first. Her son, Jonah, is only six. But he was stoked. She said Suzie has hooked up with some high finance heavy. I don't know what Laura's situation is. She was with another young woman, Lily Barth. They had driven over from Hawthorne to spend a few hours at the beach, work on their tans, and give the kids some sand castle building time. She looked good, Laura, happy, healthy, past that point where younger girls sometimes worry too much about how they look. She looked comfortable with herself. She seemed free and gentle, well off. It was nice of her to come over and say hi and ask how I was doing. I didn't recognize her at first. She was very quiet, listening, keeping one eye on me and the other eye on her kids. She had a lovely smile, and bright, green eyes. She was not afraid to let the talk die off, and she just stood there, looking at me, not in any weird or strange way, but there was no need to fill the silence with anything.

She looked at my scar. She reached out and touched it gently with her fingers.

When I think of all that has been loaded on us, given us,

shared with us, or loaned us, or that we simply took, and what we have lost or misplaced, forgotten or tossed, thirsted for, drank and spilled, or pissed out, hoarded or wasted, put away in safe deposit boxes or on shelves under glass in museums or thrown out in the nightly garbage, or buried in hope chests or sold at swap meets, pasted into scrap books or wadded up and tossed into a roadside gutter, all these things, all the debris, the rubble, the knickknacks, the statues, the holy cards and playing cards, all the prized possessions that just yesterday we were so proud of, going into debt for, polishing and spit-shining, going to war for, and of the drinks and food consumed and composted, of books bought, read, loaned, sold, donated, tossed aside, and furniture, beds and chairs and tables and nightstands and television sets and radios and paintings and photographs, of handprints and footprints set in cement, of cars and surfboards, trucks and troop carriers, boats and helicopters, of all these things that mix up and make up life, when I roll it all up, all this sweet and sour stuff into the poet's ball, I think that surfing, next to one another, next to you and me, next to you, Penina, surfing is what I value most, surfing, the ocean, the beach, close-in.

We live on this bay, our beach, prey to kooks and tourists and commercial encroachment. Surfing combines at once primal forces, needs, wants into a physical and mental activity combined into one motion of exuberance. But that excitement gives way, matures into joy and celebration. And the surfer feels a part of nature and the natural environment, and is not isolated or alienated from the physical world, from life, from sand and water and reef and cove and seaweed and birds and fish. The surfer's world is of splashing water and fearless fish, of salty sand and shell covered rocks, of cove and point, and of the swerve of the waves coming quietly into the cove, breaking off from the point and pouring onto a golden green sea grassy sandy beach.

I know what you are thinking: when will Salty grow up? You said as much. But this has nothing to do with maturing, to use your word, but with seeing through to the other side. The other side of what? What even is it that has sides?

We sometimes don't fully know the true value of something until it has been taken from us. Hell is an ocean with no waves. Henry was swimming in such a place, always paddling with a swell that was never going to break into a wave. And hell an ocean with no waves is also an apt description of war, a definition of the futility of the enterprise. When I first got back, I couldn't tell you this, or anyone. I don't want to say no one understood me, what I had been through in the war. That's a copout. There are many who understand what I experienced. War is not a mystery. War is as basic as gravity. What goes up must come down. What goes to war must be destroyed. Funny things happen in war, though, like shit running uphill, contrary to the plumber's first theorem. And there are many varieties of war experience. Ray and Mary Chippy speak to one. War impacts all of us, those who go, those who stay, those who fight, those who protest, those who run, those who jump on the grenade cliché, those who dress up, those who dress down, those who enter as privates and exit as privates, their privates exposed to the flame throwers, those who make the best of war, and those who make the worst of war, those who fight to end war, and those who fight to fight another war, and so on and so on, and so off.

Malone says I need to forget about the war. He says the years following a war are good years to grow a business, and I should concentrate on helping him grow the business. I said they are good years to grow a business if you win the war, and I'm not sure we did win the war, but he said, no, it doesn't matter who wins. All the survivors grow their businesses, he said. And probably he's right, anyway. Where did he ever get so enthused about business? I don't think he's been in the water once this week.

Funerals are for the living. That's why Henry's casket was closed. No one wanted to look at him when he was alive, why would they want to look at him melting in his own goo now that he's dead? Why did Henry kill himself? Why didn't he grab a board and paddle out? Henry didn't want to live on the water. Henry wanted to live among men. Why? Henry never did learn to surf alone. He liked surfing. Surfing for Henry was his only escape from himself. On the wave even Henry forgot about where he came from. But he never found joy in the water. He always wanted something more. And he did not know the happiness that comes from swinging a hammer, like Ray and Tom Chippy knew and shared. Why did Henry move down to the beach? Not to surf. To be near you? To show off his sports car? To roller skate?

Malone is forming a corporation, and I'm to be vice president in charge of publications. Malone sure knows how to inflate a raft. But I've talked him into publishing a monthly newsletter that I'll write. I'll also be responsible for all advertising. One of my first goals is to take down that poster from the wall over your bed, the one with all the surfers looking down at you. Just kidding. But I will be designing some new posters. And I've also talked Malone into a publishing venture, a quarterly journal of surfing and the arts. We'll solicit surf photos, surf poetry, short stories and non-fiction pieces about surfing trips up and down the coast, drawings and artwork. I'm not sure what to call it, maybe, "forth on the godly sea," from Ezra Pound's first canto, or maybe, "froth on the godless sea," but Malone said not to get too nutty. He doesn't trust poetry, and probably he's right about that, too. We're talking surfers here, he said. Remember your audience, he said. I said maybe we should call it "Penina's Letters." But he has a point, but at the same time I think he lacks the artist's vision. He's strictly a businessman. But I suppose business is an art too. Maybe we should call the journal "Surf's Flat." When the surf's flat, and you have to come out of the water, you've something to read, read about surfing, the ocean, waves, beach culture, surf spots, surf trips, new developments in surfboards and equipment. Malone said we should include a centerfold, but he didn't mean a centerfold of a surfer. I did not pursue that idea, nor will I tell you who he thought might make a good candidate for the first centerfold. Anyway, we kicked around some ideas for a title: "Foam," "Blown Out." Maybe you can give a title some thought. Let me know what you come up with. But I want the publication to be primarily a venue for writing, for literature about the ocean, waves, and beaches, nature. The first issue will include something I've written about my three days living on the Bay. Malone wants me to ghost write an introduction by him, but I'm insisting he write something in his own hand, the coward. Of course I'll still be shaping and selling boards. And we've come up with an idea for a surf camp, a school for young surfers.

I'll be busy at the shop. And surfing. Every morning of

every day, down to the water, set forth indeed on the wild and loony and lonely poet's godly godless godforsaken god gifted goddess sea, set sharpened fin to warped wave, lay waxed board down on walking water, waking water, washing water, wilting water, wasting water, still on the sea to watch the gliding birds, pelicans, gulls, cormorants, feel the fish near, roll with the jellyfish in the fog of the sounding buoys, talk to the deft dolphins swimming in the shadows of the swells, drift with the currents and tides, and converse with the slurring waves, and only later, if there's still time, set pen to paper in a new letter to Penina.

But what about this letter, the letter I'm writing to you now, and this very moment I am writing, pushing the pencil across the paper, drawing curlicues like waves, thoughts breaking into white water then receding into this moment's past, what Puck calls real time, as if there were any other kind, but by which he means not wasting time, but time well spent, not the same real time you will be reading the letter though, between which, between my writing and your reading, a thousand waves may have passed, waves this pencil will not have ridden? That was a long question, a long wave, a long ride toward some shore, but what shore? Where is this letter going? Where are we going? Where am I taking you? Where are you taking me?

About nine months ago, still in-country, I met Florence,

the old Chinese woman I told you about in a couple of letters. She gave me a book of poems with ink drawings. One of the poems was accompanied by a drawing of a man in bed, moonlight pouring through an open window onto a cold looking floor. Florence wanted me to help her work on a translation of the poem into English.

Florence's poem was by the Chinese poet Li Po. It describes being awake at night, thinking, far from home, or perhaps far from the past, thus probably rethinking the past, or what we call remembering, or reflecting. Homesickness is a kind of nostalgia, sentimental and dangerous. One feels regret, but there is no going back. Usually, in translations of Li Po's poem, there's moonlight and frost, one mistaken for the other in the night, and a mountain and a moon, a confused awakening at night with thoughts of home. Florence had many things to remember, yet was always interested in what was new.

War is waiting for a train. You feel the ground, put your ear to the rail. Away in the field you may have time to be reflective. But reflection may not be good for us. Falling asleep away from home, we are awakened by an illumination of moonlight, but in our sleepiness, we might easily confuse the light with frost, or our current bed with some other bed. The moon awakens us, and we are momentarily stupefied. We don't know where we are. Or we think we are home, but we are not home. We are far from home.

Near my bed tonight the moonlight spreads like silver paint, like desert frost across the bare wood floor, and I'm thinking again of Florence and Li Po, and I feel like writing. The moon drifts through a cloud curtain. Highland Avenue is quiet. It's late. I fall back to sleep thinking of home. I am home. There is no home.

By the moonlight's loose ice on the sill of the broken window I lift my head to see the bright brush of the streetlight down the block going from green to yellow then to red, and burning I throw away the blanket and drop my head, dreaming I am home.

Drill Sergeant Haett shakes me awake. He's laughing. "If you hadn't fallen asleep so drunk, you'd know the difference between moonlight on the floor and frost in the grass," he says. I awake with a clear mind, wind through water. This would not have happened were I in my own bed. Anyway, I don't have a bed to call my own.

Florence was an old Chinese woman. No need to be jealous. She was years and ages from her home. Every time she saw me she took out her notebook, yellow and brittle, and showed me a new poem with drawing and her own translation. "Famous poem," Florence said. "Li Po. Centuries old. I remember. I write this. Please, you read."

"Wake up! Quick! It's snowing! Will you go to work?" Florence said she asked her husband.

"Pull the sled out," he told her. But when she went out to see to the sled, the snow had disappeared.

"That's the moon on the beach. It doesn't snow here. Go back to sleep. Dream of the ocean, the desert," Florence's husband told her.

We are often awake at night, and there is never a frost. Moon white sheets cover the wet fields that rise up into the mountains.

I get back into bed thinking of the house Florence lived in for a time, near the smelter, down in the hot valley. One night my squad camped outside the house, and I dreamed of the waves in the cove and of the train above the campground, and of the cold wind in the pine trees down in the grove.

"Go back to sleep," Florence said her husband yelled at her. "It was my own stupid snoring, he say me. Quit thinking of home, he say me. It's all gone now," Florence said, laughing hard, snorting, a shriveled old woman. She might have been a hundred years old.

Is that the moon, or the streetlight, down on the corner? What difference does it make? It's a still, clear night. Streetlights move through phases. Moons don't sit still, fixed to the tops of poles. One night, an overnight pass, and four of us hopped in a jeep for a drive into town. "Is that moonlight, or black ice on the road?" the driver asked. "What's black ice?" I asked. "Whatever the hell it is, slow down," someone said. "We're almost there," the driver said. "No, we've a long ways to go."

Thinking of home I fall back to sleep and again awake thinking of home. I'm always thinking of home. The moon seeps under the door. Rising tide of light covering the floor like ice inching across the lake. In the morning the rifle oil has me thinking of home. I can smell the eucalyptus, the salt sea air, the hibiscus, sitting under the olive tree with you, Penina, in my Dad's back yard, admiring your eyes turning blue to a dark green jade in the shadows of the sunset, under the olive tree. We kiss, wet one another's lips.

Walking on the beach we picked up tar between our toes. We used the tar for glue to patch teeth in our hand made tikis, sitting under the fan palms up from the beach. Now, in a land where moon frost and light are equally cheap, I can't afford these thoughts of home, of my own bed, of sleeping with you. On my grass floor now, by my bed on the ground, wood frosted moonlight. I lift my head and the moon stirs over the trees, also awake, always awake, of course, and dead, dead light, ghostly, but the light drifting across the grass, like a buoy on water, reflecting the moon in my eyes, the light is alive and wakens the grass to the night.

I'm outside, standing in the gravel on a cold desert morning. The streetlight above the barracks is blinking as the sun comes up across the flat desert floor. We board a troop carrier and drive farther out into the desert white sands, shadows and ice across the black road. We drive all day and reach the dunes after sunset. In the dunes the moon is alive in the hills, sprinkling silver shadows across a few eucalyptus trees where we've set up camp for the night. There's a salty onshore breeze coming up over the dune. I fall asleep in my cot, dreaming of home. Moonlight paints frost on the grass floor under the tent fly.

A cold blend of moonlight and frost in the dunes awakens me. I think of home and the family, my mother and father, the empty house. I get up and walk to the top of the dune and look down on the beach and waves, the moon falling warmly over the bronze dunes. Fragments of shadow dance in the ice plant. The moon rolls across the dunes. In the morning we get up early and break camp. It's early and there's no coffee because we have to move out. Riding in the back of the troop carrier there's nothing to remind me of home. At the next stop I get into bed, a sleeping bag in the sand, thinking of home, and I can't sleep. The moonlight sticks to my eyelids like silver thaw. We are camped in a grove of old oaks, clean and cold, on a hill back up off the beach. The light on the water is frozen solid, clean and cold. Over the bay the moonlight spreads foam from a wave washing over the sand. I awake and walk out of camp down to the beach. It's a long walk. The moon throws a white blanket of cotton curling over the ocean.

Another night, and I'm to walk perimeter guard around the motor pool. In the distance I can see desert town cold lights, across the desert darkness, far beyond this perimeter. I remember a night we slept under fan palms near the water, sleeping in the sandy grass. I walk the perimeter in the early morning hours, cold. One by one the soldiers awake. There's no general call this morning. There will be coffee and eggs, and rumor tells there will be sausage and bacon. I get in the mess line. Everyone has tin cup out and ready for the coffee. It's been three days and no coffee. One by one the soldiers walk over and get into the line. The morning sun rises and touches the walls of the barracks. The mess line casts individual shadows against the yellow walls. Later, there's a mail call. Someone says they had snow in El Paso last week. Weapons are handed out, steel handled, long hair mops.

Some general is dropping by, accompanied by a senator accompanied by his staff. We're standing in a tight formation for a close inspection. One disheveled young recruit is dry shaving in formation. It's Bubo. You can hear the dry blade scrape across his frozen cheeks. I've fallen asleep on my feet, in formation. I've fallen into an abyss, my only connection to you my thoughts of home. We pass the inspection and are given leave to go into town. Nightfall, neon lights blinking in an asphalt courtyard. My drunken buddies are asleep in the motel room. They don't hear me knocking. The weekend passes, soldiers on the streets, away from their homes. Most don't appear to mind during the long weekend leave. They don't wear theirs hearts on their sleeves. They don't cry themselves to sleep. I grow frazzled from waiting and writing, from mind damaged letters full of cryptic poetry. No one seems to mind the madness of the riptides. The general issued a warning. Most of the soldiers obey the signs. The water pulls me to sea.

I think I must be allergic to moonshine. I take a nap and sleep through taps. I awake in a pool of electric light, shuddering, thinking of you. I don't know if I'm near the water or in the middle of the desert. I'm thinking of you, but are my thoughts with you? An ocean separates us. I wrote that, in a letter to you, Penina. And I imagined our bodies pulling through the water. Do you remember what you wrote back to me?

"That's silly. Go to sleep, Salty."

It was good criticism and good advice. I walk down to the water. The moon slides in under the palms. A guitarist plays. The king snake sneaks through the oak tree. An old woman carves teeth in a palm frond tiki. The moon breaks in two. Half goes with me and half with you, parting at the station. Moonlight fills my window, awakens me. I reach for you, thinking I am home.

Moonlight touches my pillow, your hand in winter. Above me stands the guard, his flashlight in my eyes. It's my turn to walk the perimeter, a loaded weapon in my hands, below the motor pool, alone in the desert moonlight, above the ocean beach.

In the motel room the soldiers take turns on the phone, calling home. The moon sparks a dull glow of coins on the bureau. The sergeant awakens, still drunk. Dizzy from the wine he's drank or the telephone ringing, past the agreed time for him to call home.

On leave again. Sitting up from a beach below hills in clouds. Cloud melts mountain. No sun, no moon in winter seen through steamed window shields. A cloud dark creeps across the steep road before the blue rain awakens thoughts of you. We stop for coffee in a clumsy café. Some kid calls "Nina!" as the waitress seats us. For a confused second I think, Penina? Lowering my head, I watch where I'm going.

Camping out under the moon at low tide up from the beach. Went walking in a nearby cove in the evening after mess. Seaweed stuck to the rocks. Pelicans, shells, cold foam curls around my legs, the waves peeling like green artichoke scales.

We've received another set of orders. The orders change almost daily. The censor won't permit any more discussion of this. More moons coming.

"Move over," I hear someone say from another tent.

"Go back to sleep."

And suddenly we're in another city and a moolish moon glows over the motel, its neon sign blinking red and blue. Go back to sleep, Penina. You are not in the motel room under this motel moon, neon sign blinking, street noise curtain. Yet you open the night sky. I know the smell of your moonflower hair drenched with salt water.

There's been an earthquake here. I dreamt I was on the water. The earthquake came at moonrise, and I am now involved in moonlighting maneuvers, working with my hands. I love working with my hands.

The moon is hiding high in a fog. I've too many thoughts. I simply can't allow these thoughts to mist my mind. The old moon's waning light waxes the floor under my bed. That floor is not solid.

Why a moon, anyway, and why just one? Why not two, as I lie awake thinking of Li Po and Florence, of Son House, and Penina's letters, too. But I'm exhausted by this moon, and the moon is tired of me, passes by. I drop my last dime into the pay

275

phone. The operator wants more. I'm out of coins. You're probably not home tonight, anyway. Invisible moon, the barracks full of moonish, molding men.

I dream I'm sitting on my board, listening in fog for the sound of waves. I awake to a silent ocean. This far away, I can't hear the surf. I fall back, longing for home.

Three days ago we were told to move out again, after a week of sitting around in a great heat, our shirts off, without much happening, writing a few letters, pulling perimeter guard duty. It was so still there wasn't even a hint of a rumor circulating. Then the order came, and we went to work quickly, commerce. We broke camp in the evening. The Bridge Platoon pulled up the bridge and loaded it onto the trucks. The moon had already fallen, and in the red hot dust of pulling up stakes, backfilling holes, getting trucks started and moved into line, I forgot about you. The moon had fallen, and the night was dark, and you were forgotten. Memory has become a kind of lust. A day of moving and now we are set up near a creek bed. The bridge is down. In the bright moonlight my bed floats, a swamped boat in storm surf. I grab at the sheets, fall to the deck, come quickly about, awake in this odd tent.

Another day and another mail call. I receive a letter from you. Your heart never seems to turn. I have not seen its dark side.

The moon opens and closes on your white letter. I can see blue swells rising in the distance, behind your writing, and green and white waves falling. The motor pool yard is gorged with light. We've put some grass in for a makeshift ballpark. We will play under the lights tonight. The generator truck is up and running. Again this dream thought of falling with the white water in the night.

Another furlough, and the light surrounds us. From my bed in the motel room I lift my head. It's the glow the television emits. I look at my watch. Hours of restless motel sleep. There's only one channel on the TV that works, and I watch some state sponsored soap opera. I don't know what the characters are saying.

Seashells smashed into sand in storm surf. The animal has abandoned the shell. The shell of my heart is empty. Empty, this feeling away from home. In uneasy sleep, bright dreams unearth our parting with moonlight that pulls like a riptide our hearts to sea. I awaken early to see the mountain still covered with clouds. I'm reminded of El Porto hidden across the beach from the path, waves in fog.

They've given me a week for some rest and relaxation. I could go home for a day or two, but I fear I could not come back again, so I don't want to go home, not now. It's a cheap shot, their telling me I can go home. I'd have to catch my own military hop, an uncertain schedule, and dependent on orders that change daily. I talk to a short hop specialist. He says he can get me on a plane to an island not too far away. He tells me I might be able to surf for a couple of days. But the doctor told me not to get the stitches wet.

I arrive in the city to find homes lit greenly, lights red, blue, gold, festively flashing, green, red, blue, yellow, white, and stars falling over the mountain. Artificial lights in a warm dark night. Paper lanterns. I make my way to a motel in a crowded part of the city. I mention surf spots to the cab driver. He doesn't seem to know what I'm talking about. I fall asleep without food or drink. I dream of waves rolling up the streets, washing away cars, water rising everywhere, into homes, people swimming in fear, swimming in the streets, no escaping, no escaping a moonlight as bright as an explosion.

I'm sitting one at a table for two on a sidewalk café in a crowded part of the city, a few blocks from my motel, though I'm not sure I'll be able to find my way back. I write a poem on a napkin:

Moon so big
Heart won't fit
Li Po sang
Take another sip.

Big fat moon
Fitless heart
This song I sing
Time to part.

I drank too much, and now I'm sleeping on the moon, my flashlight near my cot, the campfire cold. Dew appears, far below, earth, blue white and snow dark shadows. I awake to the sound of dogs barking out on the street. Next door there are some young people partying. My room is dark and hot. It's summer here, and there is no air conditioning. I wait until the moon rises, and I go out and wander the streets. I find my way down to a beach, a small cove. I think I see a seal head popping up, out of purple water. I must be hallucinating from the rancid local beer. I was drinking it from a tap. I should have stuck to bottles, but they didn't look new, but refilled. I touch the water in the cove and remember how the salt dried on your skin, making the little hairs on your arms stand stiff and white. I lick up the salt across your closed eyelids. The moon is in the cove. The night is cooling some. I fall asleep in the sand near the water. I dream that I am a lost surfer caught in seaweed beds. The lifeguards are out looking for me. I catch abalone but the shells are empty. I see you sleeping up on the beach under the fan palms, up from the water, above the fat waves, below a streetlamp moon. I awake and find my way back to my motel room. The city is finally quiet. On the wall above my bed is a cheap picture of a dirty wave. I remember Jack on the beach after escaping in the crowded boat, looking for bodies on the beach in the light of a bloated moon.

I remember Bubo and his bloated penis.

There's nothing to do on this rest and relaxation furlough but walk, find a sidewalk café table, drink, and write poem letters to you on napkins. I feel like going for a lunar swim. I remember Sergeant Williams's instructions as he handed me my furlough.

"Stick to the path, Salty," he said. "Don't wander off dreaming. Realize the traps away from home, away from your buddies. If anyone stops you, don't forget your purpose, and never forget your family, home, waiting for you."

The path to this motel room is covered with laughing leaves. I toss my street map into a trashcan. In a single block half a dozen prostitutes proposition me. I smile politely and keep walking. The way is strewn with fools drinking stale wine. Once you leave home you don't know the way. Away from family, no way to go.

In the morning I walk back down to the little cove and watch some local fishermen taking a boat out. I would like to help them and to go with them, paddle out onto the water. The boat breaks the water, and they brush through the small foamy waves in the protected cove. I spend most of the day hanging around the fishermen's beach camp. I try to talk to a few. They know what I am. Still, they are patient with me. They are patient men.

Back in my motel room I think I hear a tambourine jangling, and I hear music like at a roadhouse. I think of moving to a better place, a hotel, a place of moon skin plum peels and expensive wine purple sheets. I imagine you are at home asleep under covers of thin green water. But I remember it is not summer in your home, and you are full of cold-drawn music, steely guitars, and bossy tambourines. From the party next door I hear what sounds like sticks and skateboards, wheels and harmonicas. I'm restless. I get up and walk in a direction I've not yet explored. I reach an edge of town. A train trundles across a trestle. The ground trills, and the palms shiver. I discover another cove. An early morning fisherman pauses and waves. The waves pause, like they pause just before an explosion then reverse and start to break backwards.

I watch a group of students in uniform, homeward bound, caps pulled forward, satchels stuffed with books. They pass my sidewalk café table, their faces full of curiosity toward the exiled poet. They can see he's a poet from his stack of used napkins, but he's not eating. He's drinking and drawing pictures.

No exit, no way out of here. The military hop that was supposed to take me back to my unit failed to show. I spent the last 24 hours hanging around a Quonset hut waiting for new orders. Neither yesterday's nor tomorrow's rain waters today's flowers. In some other place this moon will not follow you. Some other moon will peek longingly and shyly across a fern fronded forested ocean beach. The men are all talking of home, of family, of work. Of home I can't speak honestly. I haven't been there lately, nor have I heard from family. I try to explain. I don't have a family. But there is a girl waiting for me. The talk drifts back to the war. War is work, tools and desks, trucks, fields and mountains and beaches, towns and bars and girls. Someone is talking about his sisters. I don't remember any sisters or brothers, father or mother, and I've never had a wife. Fog and darkness descending on the still hot asphalt of the short tarmac. Heavy dressed pilots walking toward some helicopters, walking with their orders. The tarmac begins to shine black as the fog falls down.

I've been talking with one of the helicopter pilots. He's returning home after 16 months flying missions. He's afraid he'll return a stranger to his community and to his self. He asks to see my notebook. "What are you writing?" He glances through a few pages and hands it back to me, shaking his head. "I don't know, man."

I take a sand dune path away from the tarmac and walk down to a beach. There's a small harbor, colorful towels hanging from open windows. Where the moon leaves the path I hear dark cracking, like tree limbs breaking. Someone is building a campfire down on the beach.

The moon blossoms through clouds over the mountain. Lost on the moon, looking for a path, the way home, enormous fungus, trees smothered with mold. Wet, dark foggy patches. What an old place, this far off the path.

Music on the moon. Someone is playing a flute. No wind. Clear notes suspended. What incredible sustain! Life on the moon, alone from home, cold moon fire, below earth train.

I receive new orders. I'm to wait here until my unit returns from a night problem. This may take a few more days. I walk back to town, pick a new motel, go for a walk in another part of town I've not explored. I come across a group of nuns singing. Full habits like ornaments rising above their caroling blue voices. I almost forgot. It's Christmas time. Seems so odd, Christmas in summer. The ascension of the small choir after the rise they fall one by one like snow petals like cherry blossoms. No, it's not Christmas. It's Easter, passion week.

What will stop this repetition, this moon mood.

A hollow fragile moon like a falling leaf in the palm at the end of the beach. In the cove before the evening swells cool, swimming through kelp beds at high tide below the gentle cliffs. A few of the local fishermen are diving for abalone. I join them. On the beach a bonfire. I drift around the point and come ashore at the bottom of a steep cliff. I join their little campout up above the beach. The train rattles over the trestle above the campground. Moonlight paints silver the shaking black rails. A tree snake smokes safely through a mangrove tree, swaddled in spottled red and black and yellow.

At moonrise the waves fold into themselves, froth and foam, a briny salt mud washes up the beach. Sand crabs come up in the bubbles and go bubbling down head first into the wet sand. There are children running about chasing fish, a salty sandy grunion, with flashlights and noise and moonglow. I remember our Refugio nights.

I walk back to my motel room, falling off the moon onto the hard linoleum floor waxed to a golden honey shine. The floor reminds me of an old surfboard smeared with wax. The moon bead necklace like light oil washes your skin. This old linoleum floor, like the floors of barracks, empty barracks, the bunks decommissioned, a detail waxing the floor, and in the plastic tiles I see your face. How can that be?

In your small room in the back of the garage under the olive and jade and the scarlet bougainvillea coming through the open window and your blue eyes and wet sand yellow hair and someone is singing about a night on the way, a night full of empty sky.

Through my motel window moonlight spills frost over the dark linoleum floor. Red and blue neon light blinking in the street. I can't seem to escape the moon's reach, the moon's pull, the moon's push. I get up and go out and walk into the bowl of the cove, moonlight pouring over palms and waves and wet rocks. On the beach around a fire in the sand, musical instruments, and a girl with chlorine green hair. They are drinking and singing. The girl joins the singing, and dances in circles, her white pony grazing in the moonlight in the dark green grass. I brought my own bottle of wine with me down to the beach. The moon is wearing a white dress and riding a bicycle and in the night falls prey to the drinkers. The moon disappears into the crowd. I fall asleep on the beach, under clouds of green bottles. I awake to loud noises, singing, waves crashing. No one notices the silence of the rising night tide, such is the clamor around the fire of the tambourines, wood flutes, and guitars. Drinking wine in the moonlight, banging on some green guitars with the locals, until a wave's blue drunk drowns our beach fires.

In the red tide at Refugio we drew our first names in the soft wet sand, moonbeam lighting across the bay. We swam in the green phosphorescent foam.

I try to sleep the night through, but the local lunatics are banging pots and pans outside my door. They want the soldier boy to come out and play some more. A firecracker pops in my room. The local cops arrive. I hope the MPs don't hear of the problem.

Eating red potatoes, drinking white wine, something slept the night on the small carpet outside my room.

My new orders have finally arrived. I'm standing in a field jacket starched in formation, an interpretation, mail call, knees unlocked. There's a waving wind, and the heat is rising off the tarmac. I've a dozen letters from you, held up during my furlough.

Back in the field. Near my cot, frost on the bare grass. I reach out of my bag and touch the scorching light, far from home.

Policing cigarette butts at dawn in the yard of a Monterey sunrise, pink and blue valley sky. In the dark barracks the dog-tired soldiers sleep, unaware of the moon's passing over the ocean. We're all being discharged. I've arranged a hop down to Los Angeles.

My last night, a warm night sitting with some guys under the green pepper trees on the base. An old sergeant is playing a blues on a steel guitar, and one of the cooks brings over a cardboard box full of red tomatoes and passes them around with a jar of salt. We're drinking wine coolers. In a distant barracks a rusty radio plays happy rock and roll. I think of being with you tomorrow night, eating oranges and drinking on the beach in the moonlight. There are cherry blossoms here, the petals whirling about like falling snow, the bees still buzzing, restless. The men are happy, acting silly. There's a pause as someone remembers a buddy left behind. I mention Bubo, how we had planned to hop out together, but he got sick. I had not heard from him. He would be okay. I had not abandoned him in the field. I left him in the infirmary.

I fear I have lost my way. I am on a dangerous path, no path, lost in the green shadows, trying to find my way out. Words pile up. What a waste. Not one of these letters describes my true longing for you. I go to bed, my last night without you. I see the green sheer water curling about your body surfing the blue shards.

It's early morning and I climb into the back of a troop carrier taking us to the airfield where we've all arranged military hops throughout the day. The bulbous moon is broken into little pieces glittering in the oil soaked wood in the bed of the truck carrying off the quiet soldiers. I see children swimming in the waves of a sunny cove, a dappling breeze through the empty palms. Fresh, new waves roll flashing white into the rocks at the edge of the beach. Thoughts beginning to thaw, reading newspaper clippings, old letters, soldiers talking over worn pictures, talking about plans, what we will do when we get home, who will meet us at the airport. The guy sitting next to me has never seen his 13-month-old baby boy.

My hop is delayed another night. I sleep on the armory floor. The moonlight drifts like smoke near the beach. Through a silk cloud curtain, moonlight spreads. I fall back to sleep, silver paint spilling across the cement floor. Images, remembrances, dangle in and out, off and on, in my mind, half awake, half dreaming, a house, a beach, a song, a woman, a wave. I fall asleep. When I awake again, an hour or so later, a cold frost now sticks across the bare concrete floor. I slowly trace in the frost the letters of your name. Penina. It's not frost on the floor. It's sand, warm sand. Beach dust.

I remember the lines of distant swells rolling slowly into waves we used to read from the dunes above the cove, watching clutters of seabirds lifting and falling like cloth napkins and confetti whiffling down toward the water.

Love, Salty

~ ~ ~

Joe Linker attended El Camino College and California State University at Dominguez Hills, completing a BA in English, with a minor in 20th Century Thought and Expression, and an MA in English, while putting in six years in the Army California National Guard. Two decades of adjunct work bookend 25 years in what Han-shan called the "red dust" of business (CPCU, 1992). He was a Hawthorne Fellow at the Attic Institute of Arts and Letters, Summer 2012.

The author thanks Emily for typing a very early draft of Penina's Letters back when she was in high school, John for reading and commenting on a more recent draft, his Hawthorne Fellows cohort, and Susan, who knows a good letter when she reads one.

CPSIA information can be obtained at www.ICGtesting.com
Printed in the USA
LVOW11s0811170616

492919LV00003BA/194/P

9 781530 686889